A ZHONG FONG
MYSTERY

THE HAMLET
MURDERS

A ZHONG FONG
MYSTERY

THE HAMLET MURDERS

DAVID ROTENBERG

McArthur & Company
Toronto

First published in Canada in 2004 by
McArthur & Company
322 King St. West, Suite 402
Toronto, Ontario
M5V 1J2
www.mcarthur-co.com

National Library of Canada Cataloguing in Publication

Rotenberg, David (David Charles)
The Hamlet murders / David Rotenberg.

"A Zhong Fong mystery".
ISBN 1-55278-410-X

I. Title.

PS8585.O84344H34 2004   C813'.54   C2003-907489-7

Jacket design, f/x / Composition: *Mad Dog Design*
Author Photo: *John Reeves*
Printed in Canada by *Friesens*

The publisher would like to acknowledge the financial support of
the Government of Canada through the Book Publishing Industry
Development Program, the Canada Council for the Arts, and the Ontario
Arts Council for our publishing activities. We also acknowledge the
Government of Ontario through the Ontario Media Development
Corporation Ontario Book Initiative.

10 9 8 7 6 5 4 3 2 1

For my father, Dr. Cyril Rotenberg,
whose quiet support was always there
and always greatly appreciated

Acknowledgements

I'd like to thank my brilliant translator and friend Ms. Zhang Fang for all her help with the novel. As well, I'd like to acknowledge the much-valued advice I received from my readers and support that Michael and Kim have offered me. And, as always, my thanks to my friends, brothers, Susan, Joey and Beth – without whose patience and inspiration no book could possibly come to completion.

CONTENTS

CHAPTER ONE

THE INSIDER'S PRICE

It started with Fong in the shower, naked and covered in soap, when the water in his rooms on the grounds of the Shanghai Theatre Academy suddenly, for no apparent reason, just stopped. It ended with four people dead, one unaccounted for and love in tatters. But love, even torn and shredded and stomped on like something disgusting that crawled out of a sewer grate on Fuxing Donglu – even just the hope of love – remained the only thing that made getting out of bed in the morning worth the bother, whether there is any water in the shower or not. And love, even in the secular kingdom of the People's Republic of China, still needed a miracle to lure it out of the dark cool shadows into the hot light of day – especially in the intense heat and humidity that is August in Shanghai.

Fong pushed aside the shower curtain and reached for a towel, and because he could see even less than usual with the soap in his eyes, he actually missed it. On his second attempt, he grabbed the towel, scraped the soap off his chest and then shouted, "*Wo cao!!!*" to no one in particular.

"Such language," the ancient house warden shouted back from the courtyard outside his window. "And who exactly is it that you want to tickle your privates, Detective Zhong?" The crone cackled at her own cleverness then added, "Those renovations before the condo conversion you voted for are coming along just fine, don't you think?" More of her throaty laughter came next, then a choking sound, then a horking and finally the distinct sound of something moist splatting to the cracked courtyard pavement.

Fong tried the taps a second time – no water. He was going to swear again, but really, what was the point? He wrapped the towel around his waist then headed back into the bedroom. Opening the blinds, he saw two paunchy white men wearing expensive raw silk jackets, the backs of which were turned up at odd angles like the pages of a paperback novel left out in the rain. Bum wings, the Shanghanese called them. As Fong wondered what idiots would bother with raw silk in the sweltering reality of a Shanghai summer, one of the men pulled a set of blueprints from a long tube and unfurled it. "Ah, contractors," Fong thought. The man began gesticulating with his arms as if he had stepped on an open 220-volt line. Fong revised his assessment, "Ah, French contractors." The French, Fong found, often spoke no Mandarin and only very bad English. For some reason, they expected people in the Middle Kingdom to learn French. Why? There were one point three billion of us, how many were there of them?

Before he could answer that question, a middle-aged Han Chinese male emerged from the scene shop across the way with a steaming jar of tea. No doubt he was the Frenchmen's Beijing keeper. Foreigners tended to look on their keepers as tour guides. They aren't. They are ranking party officials who keep tabs on the comings and goings of powerful foreigners in the People's Republic of China. The Beijing keeper turned his head. Almost the entirety of his left cheek and much of his chin was covered by a dark raspberry-coloured stain. Florid stain, bad suit, worse teeth, and probably enough power to have whole areas of the city closed down with a single phone call. Looking at the trio, Fong grinned. They sure deserved each other. All they had to do was add a full-dress mullah – are there any other kind – to make a full deck, or whatever the proper name was for a complete set of incompetent but powerful morons.

Then Fong noticed that the Henry Moore–esque statue, which had contaminated his view in the courtyard for many years, had been turned around. He squinted to be sure he was right. He was. Now the round hole, instead of the abundant curve, faced Fong's rooms. Who would bother to turn the stupid thing around? For a moment, Fong wondered if that meant that the drunken student actors who frequented the statue would be closer to his rooms or farther away. In either case, they were too close.

Could this really be the beginning of the threatened renovations that were to precede the conversion of his building to condos? Water off, statue moved, three grownup idiots in the courtyard – yep, this could be it.

If it was, then this was the day that Fong had dreaded. He had been offered the "special insider's price" to buy his rooms, but this was still way beyond his means. And he couldn't leave here. It was here that he had known his first wife, Fu Tsong. Known her. Loved her. Come alive with her. He couldn't even think about leaving here. These rooms had been Fu Tsong's. Then they had belonged to both of them. Then just to him. But these rooms would always be Fu Tsong's and he knew it – and gloried in it – too much. And he knew that too.

As he dragged his pants on, he reminded himself that it was only money – something that two of the three idiots in the courtyard, unlike himself, probably had. Then again, he had clothing appropriate to Shanghai's summer and they clearly did not. For now, that would have to be enough.

His phone rang. "*Dui.*"

The mincing voice on the other end of the line was an annoyance from his past, a Party hack's son or cousin or nephew or pimple or something, who evidently had been reassigned to Special Investigations. Fong had managed to get him moved elsewhere years ago, but clearly he had returned like a bad yuan note. Back then, Fong had dubbed him Shrug and Knock and restricted the man's communication to shrugging his shoulders and knocking on his desk. This phone call was evidence that the man's communication boundaries had been breached.

"What is it?" Fong asked.

"A reminder, Detective Zhong. It's eye time."

Fong flipped open his desk calendar and groaned. His departmentally mandated eye exam was today. He had avoided it for months even though he knew it was getting harder and harder for him to read reports, let alone the morning paper.

"You're to be at the Ukrainian Eye Centre on time and a full report is to be submitted in triplicate to the commissioner's office. Have a nice day, Detective Zhong."

Every time this man talked, Fong felt like he was chewing tinfoil. Fong reminded himself that behind Shrug and Knock's nasty façade was an even nastier self, so he should watch his step. He made a mental note to inform Captain Chen to watch his mouth around this snake, then he checked the eye doctor's address and headed out into the already scorching morning heat – toward his ocular fate.

CHAPTER TWO

VANITY FAIR AND FOUL

A hand-painted sign on the oddly coloured blue-and-yellow door read: *Ukrainian Eye Centre—Because Ukrainians Look Best.* A plaque to one side of the door proclaimed: *Only a Free Ukraine Makes Moscow Think Twice.* Fong read the signs a second time just to be sure that his failing eyes hadn't misled him. They hadn't. He rang the bell. The door opened. A large white man in a double-breasted blue blazer stood there; apparently he was Ukrainian. A Ukrainian in Shanghai? What was a Ukrainian doing in Shanghai? And he was not just white, he was the whitest person that Fong had ever seen. And round. Not a single angle on him anywhere. And to top it off, pear-shaped.

He did something with his face that Fong took for a smile, held out his pudgy white hand and said in truly awful Mandarin, "I'm Dr. Morris Wasniachenko. You can call me Dr. Wasniachenko, if that's easier for you."

Fong looked at the man and couldn't help smiling. Was he for real? Was that Mandarin he was speaking? If it was, it was the most unusual approach to the language he had ever heard. In English, Fong asked, "Do you speak English?" The man looked at Fong as if he had morphed into something really peculiar and very small. Perhaps a baby mouse.

As close as Fong could guess, the next thing the man said was, "Do you not speak the common tongue?" Before Fong could attempt an answer, the man pulled a short white jacket over top of his blazer and lit a cigarette. "D'ya mind?" he asked, Fong guessed in reference to the cigarette, not the jacket. "Well, do you speak the common tongue?" This time Fong was sure that was what he asked.

"I speak it. What is it that you're speaking?" Fong asked on impulse.

The man made a sound that may well have been laughter. Of course, it could also have been the preamble to some sort of Ukrainian folk dance. A Ukrainian in Shanghai. A Ukrainian eye doctor. How the fuck had he, the head of Special Investigations for the entire Shanghai district, ended up here? The guy must have given the department a group rate or something.

Dr. Wasniachenko parked himself on a stubby black stool that he had rigged up on wheels. Then he used his feet to trolley over to a tiny desk. His butt hung over all sides. He pulled open a tiny drawer in the desk and took out a pair of thick glasses, put them on and looked at Fong again. Fong smiled. A visually challenged Ukrainian eye doctor! The man turned and raised his head very high so that he was looking down his bulbous nose at Fong as if trying to get the glasses to focus properly for him. Then he barked out, "You're not Mrs. Jian!"

Fong laughed out loud and wondered who in his office had set this appointment up for him. He would have to return the favour in kind sometime and very soon.

"You don't look like Mrs. Jian," the good doctor said, suddenly concerned. Then his cell phone rang. He checked his pants pocket for it – no phone, his jacket pockets – no phone. "They're so small I constantly misplace them," he said as he pulled open a battered old briefcase.

Fong walked over and picked up the bright pink phone that

was sitting in the very centre of the man's desktop and handed it to the doctor. The man's fat fingers barely fit on the phone's face, but he did manage, probably through good fortune, to hit the Receive button. Instantly, his face took on a concerned look and his heavy head waggled up and down several times somewhat like an overripe tomato on the vine. Then he said, "Hold on just a second, Mom," and put the phone down. He indicated that Fong should sit in the big red chair.

Fong did and the doctor came up very close to him, "You're not Mrs. Jian?"

"No."

"Do you know Mrs. Jian?"

"There are probably several hundred thousand Mrs. Jians in Shanghai, but I'm afraid I don't know any of them."

This seemed to greatly concern Dr. Wasniachenko. He tut-tutted, made a face, turned back to Fong as if he were going to check the facts one more time, then evidently decided against it. "My mother's on the phone," he said as if that needed to be further explained. "I'm very fond of my mother. Besides my wife Tsu-li, who died seven years ago last April, she's the only woman I've ever loved. And she loves me too."

Fong was genuinely touched by the odd man's blunt candour. He found it refreshing. "You should speak to her."

The man nodded sagely several times then took out a small dark bottle with a dropper top. He trolleyed over to Fong while he held the bottle at full arm's length so that he could focus on it properly. "Open your eyes wide, Mr. Jian."

Fong did and instantly wished he hadn't because the doctor squeezed the dropper, letting loose a flood of murky brown liquid that found one eye, the entirety of his nose and dribbled down his chin. "Very good," Dr. Wasniachenko said. "Now open the other, that would be the right eye."

It wasn't, but Fong didn't see the point of contradicting the man so he opened the other eye, the left one. This time the doctor's aim was true. "Now close your eyes and stay like that. The medication takes about ten minutes to take effect. I'm going to talk to my mother. She's on the phone. Now where did I put that darned thing?"

Ten minutes later, the doctor trolleyed back into the examination room announcing, "That was my mother on the phone." Fong was going to reply, but the words stuck in his throat as he looked at the man. He was huge. Then Fong realized that the man's inordinate size must be the result of some sort of process induced by the medication that had been put in his eyes.

"Ever had your eyes tested before, Mr. Jian?"

"No," Fong said, cowering back just a little from this gigantic white person.

"So you're a virgin?" he said and giggled. Then the giggle exploded into a full-fledged belly laugh. Quickly, Fong found himself laughing too, although for the life of him he couldn't say why. This man was a walking absurdity. Then Dr. Wasniachenko flipped off the lights and turned on a projector that threw letters onto a small mirror and from there onto a wall across the way. "Can you see the letter configuration?"

"You mean the letters on the wall?" Fong asked.

The doctor took off his glasses to get a better look. In doing so, he stepped between Fong and the letters. "Yes, the ones on the wall. Read me the big letter on the top."

"I can't . . . "

But before Fong could explain that he wasn't able to see the letters through the good doctor's body, the man began that tut-tutting thing again. "Serious. Very serious," he said as he leaned in to take a close look at Fong. To do this, he moved out of the way and Fong read the whole chart from top to bottom.

"Amazing. From nothing to everything. I've only seen one other case like this. A case of hysterical near-sightedness. At first she could see almost nothing. Hardly a darn thing. Then I approached her and all at once gazzammo and she could see.

Like Christ with the lepers. Things falling off here and there, a leg, an arm, a nose and then gazzammo and those body parts back in place and they were ready to make blini."

Fong sat there completely amazed by this man. All he could think of saying was, "What was the woman's name?"

And of course the answer to his question was "Mrs. Jian." Fong nodded, and the doctor asked, "Do you know her?"

"No."

"Nice woman. You'd like her. She's Chinese, you know." Fong nodded again, but the doctor caught his head in his fleshy hands and moved a square machine toward him. He took a slightly soiled handkerchief out of his pocket and put it on the metal strut that faced Fong. "Put your chin on that." Fong did. "Now keep your eyes wide open." Fong did. The doctor sat down on the other side of the contraption. "Look at the green light." There was no green light but there was a red one so Fong looked at that although it was all the way at the upper periphery of his vision.

The doctor looked through his end of the machine and muttered loudly, "Where the hell are his darned eyes?" As he did, Fong heard the cranking of turning knobs and the red light disappeared above his line of vision. "Darn and darn again!" The doctor stood up, walked over to Fong and looked at the machine and Fong's eye. He drew a line in the air between the machine's opening and Fong's eye then hustled back to his chair. Knobs were cranked again and the red light descended from on high, stopping exactly level with Fong's right eye. "Gotch you, you little rascal. Now open your eye wide."

Fong did.

The doctor hit a button and a puff of air struck Fong square in the eyeball. Fong let out a quick gasp. "Bull's-eye. Yes, ladies and gentlemen, I've still got it. Yes, indeed. Son of a Cossack never loses his aim." Then it was as if he realized that Fong was in the room. "Did that hurt, Mr. Jian?"

"No, it just startled me a little."

"Well, they tell you to inform the patient what you're going to do before you do it, but I never believed in that. Now open your other eye."

It took several more tries – one puff went right up Fong's left nostril – but eventually the doctor completed that part of the examination.

"Good. Very good. You're sure you haven't done this before? Be honest now." But before Fong could respond, the doctor moved the clunky square machine out of the way and dropped in a heavy metal apparatus that perched on Fong's nose and covered his eyes. Dr. Wasniachenko began to flick the lenses so that Fong's vision went from acute to almost non-existent. Then the doctor put a black lens in front of Fong's left eye and touched a switch on the machine. Immediately, a line of words came up. "Can you read that?"

"I took my shoes to the cobbler."

"Very good. Good, now watch the words." He twisted some dials and the sentence split in two, the part on the left higher than the part on the right. Then the good doctor took a much-used chopstick that seemed to have the remains of a bean sprout stuck to the end of it and began to wave it back and forth in front of Fong's eyes, "Just tell me when the two parts of the sentence align with one another. I mean when they are side by side. You could think of them as forming one long line. So that they would say 'I took my shoes to the cobbler.' If you get my meaning."

Fong had got his meaning long ago but was unable to get a word in edgewise so the part that had been higher was now lower and they had to do the whole thing again. This time it worked fine, although Fong had trouble not laughing at the image of this large, round, doughy man sitting on a small stool with wheels moving a dirty chopstick back and forth very rapidly, the remains of the bean sprout moving in counterpoint to the stick.

Forty minutes, two more protestations that he had never met Mrs. Jian, and seven times being called Mr. Jian later and the good doctor informed Fong that he needed to wear glasses. What he called corrective lenses.

It had never occurred to Fong that he would need glasses. And even more important, it had never occurred to him that his vanity would resist the very idea.

Dr. Wasniachenko finished writing out a prescription just as Fong's cell phone rang. Fong flipped it open, "*Dui.*" He listened for a moment, then got up as he said, "Where exactly?" He put on his coat saying, "Cordon it off. I want to get in before Li Chou, okay?"

Fong rushed out, leaving the prescription for his glasses between two of Dr. Wasniachenko's plump fingers.

"Yet another victory for vanity – just the reason we Ukrainians lost our freedom to the Russians," the good doctor thought.

But Dr. Wasniachenko was not as addled as he appeared. While he popped the prescription into an envelope and jotted Fong's address on the outside, he phoned the Office of the Commissioner of Police for the Shanghai District and informed the duty officer there that Detective Zhong Fong would have to wear prescription lenses if he was to stay on the force. True, it was not until three days later that he remembered the prescription in the envelope, and not until two days after that that he got around to delivering it.

CHAPTER THREE

The white man's left cheek was pressed hard against the green blotter that covered the centre of his chrome-and-glass desk. The blotter had done, with admirable efficiency, what blotters are designed to do. Of course, it was blood, not ink, that had been sucked into and then successfully held by the porous fibres of the material.

Fong looked at the small weapon on the floor beside the dead man. "Guns," he thought, but resisted the impulse to kick it aside. Fong hated guns and hadn't fired one, even on a practice range, since his fluke shot had felled the Chinese-American arsonist who called himself Angel Michael. Fong actually found guns to be stupid. They made very bad hammers and only adequate paperweights. What they were good at – in fact, all they could do – was kill. Even little guns like the one on the floor beside his foot.

Fong took a pen from his shirt pocket and used it to tilt the dead man's head, exposing a tiny exit wound beneath the now tattered right earlobe. The small calibre of the bullet had caused little damage on its voyage in one ear and out just below the other. This guy was lucky to have managed to kill himself with such a narrow projectile. If lucky was the right word – and, if in fact, he had killed himself.

Fong told the other officers crowding the room to leave but signalled Captain Chen to stay. Chen took a small digital camera from his pocket and began to collect images. Fong liked this country cop he'd met way out at Lake Ching, although it was somewhat more complicated now that Chen was married to Fong's ex-wife, Lily, and was stepfather to his daughter, Xiao Ming.

Fong fished the dead man's wallet out from a coat pocket and checked his ID. "He's an American."

"Should I notify the consulate, sir?" Chen asked, taking out a pad and pencil.

There was a time in Fong's life when he would have responded with a jibe about Americans' desire to be first to know everything about everything, but he was past that. "Not yet." Chen looked up from his notepad. "They don't need to know just yet, Captain Chen."

Fong moved behind the large desk at which the dead man sprawled – and would sprawl forever if he were not moved – then turned back to the room. It was a small office in one of the dozens of gleaming new towers in the Pudong. But it was hardly elegant. "What's the nameplate on the office door say, Chen?"

Chen opened the door to check then turned back to Fong. "I can't tell, it's in English."

"Sorry," said Fong as he moved to the door. "International Exchange Institute. Pretty neutral, I'd say. Like calling a street Avenue Road."

Chen didn't laugh. He still didn't know when he was allowed to laugh in Fong's presence. All he could think of saying was, "Do they exchange money?"

"Not in any normal sense or they would have been registered with our office. Special Investigations looks after banking, as well as crimes against foreigners."

"I know, sir. So what do they exchange?"

Fong thought about that for a moment then dismissed the question and returned to the body. The cops in Forensics weren't happy when Fong insisted on being left alone with bodies, especially if he got to the crime site before them. "Just more turf wars in the department. Just the desire to identify exactly who owns which box. Tough," he thought as he canted his head toward Chen. The younger man crossed over to him. The two of them gently lifted the dead man from the desktop and leaned him back in the overly large chair. The man's features were rounded, his nose tinted a bright red from an array of tiny broken blood vessels. Fong felt the material of the jacket – very fine, very expensive even for foreigners in Shanghai. He checked for the label and made a note, a Hong Kong private tailor. Then he looked at the man's hands. Heavy, beefy and deeply calloused. He turned to Chen.

"Expensive suit, but worker's hands," said the younger man.

Fong nodded. A quizzical look crossed Chen's face, or at least Fong thought that was what that look was.

Fong pulled aside the dead man's tie and unbuttoned his shirt. He paused for a beat, then quickly rolled up the man's shirtsleeves and pant legs. Not an inch of the exposed skin was free from the tattoo artist's needle. "Find out the style. See if it was local. It may have been Hong Kong, like the suit."

Chen started to photograph the skin art.

"Who heard the gunshot?"

"His secretary."

"She's here?"

"Drinking downstairs in a bar."

"We let her . . . ?"

"She called us from there. I put an officer at the door." Fong nodded and began to move about the room again.

Chen had worked with Fong several times since Lake Ching and knew the procedure. Fong prowled and Chen waited. Finally feeling he had waited long enough, Chen asked, "Should I bring her up?"

"No. Bars are just as good for interrogations as offices."

"It's a suicide, right?"

Fong wanted to agree but he was troubled by the calibre of the gun. He was troubled by a big man even owning such a small gun. It was a woman's gun. Fong was also troubled by a man committing suicide. In China, suicide was a woman's choice. More often a countrywoman's choice. Most often accomplished by swallowing the omnipresent clear colourless pesticide provided by the government. But then again this was an American urban male, not a Chinese rural female. Fong gently returned the man's head to its original position on the desk. "Call in Li Chou's Crime Scene Unit and Forensics. And get our business folks on this. I want to know exactly what the International Exchange Institute does."

Chen nodded and headed out. Fong waited a moment to take in the place one more time. New. Clean. Sterile. Western. And a big guy with a small bullet that went in his left ear and out the right side of the head, taking off the earlobe. The bullet had created a small hole in the cheap drywall across the room and was probably lodged, if they were lucky, in the under lath. If they were unlucky, it had hit a strut and shattered. But then again, who needs the bullet? We have the gun and the fingerprints on the gun, if there are any.

A big, white beefy guy put a tiny gun into his left ear and pulled the trigger. Suicide. Not murder.

Then Fong looked at the man's date book – and a darkness crossed his face.

The woman sitting on the high barstool looked as much hooker as secretary to Fong's eyes. She wore a small sheer black top with spaghetti straps over her lovely shoulders. The tops of her patterned silk stockings weren't completely covered by the short skirt. She identified herself as a personal assistant to the deceased.

Her English was passable, but Fong decided to ask his questions in Mandarin. "How long have you worked for Mr. Clayton?"

"Bob, you mean," she corrected him.

"Do I?"

"His name is Bob."

"While we're busy correcting each other, your use of the present tense in reference to Mr. Clayton is inappropriate, one could say, wrong, since he is now dead." That quieted her for a moment. She reached for her drink but Fong beat her to it and pushed it aside. She dead-eyed him and he dead-eyed her right back. She reached for her bag on the bar and withdrew a long cigarette. "Do you mind?" she asked, clearly not giving a shit if he minded or not.

He didn't mind. Who minds a beautiful woman smoking a cigarette?

"Did Mr. Clayton smoke too?"

A burp of laughter exploded from her mouth.

"What's funny?"

"He was trying to cut back. He was worried about his health." This last was interrupted by a spluttering laugh that ended with her snorting. Pretty woman smoking, fine; snorting, not so good.

"So what exactly did you do for Bob?"

For a moment, Fong thought she was going to respond by listing sexual positions and precise bedroom activities, then he saw that she got the meaning of his question and said, "Typing, filing, girl stuff."

"Did you do his tattoos?"

She stopped, her cigarette midway to her mouth, sighed then said, "If only. They are beautiful, aren't they?"

Fong nodded, choked down his desire to ask her for a

smoke and said, "You were lovers."

Without flinching, she responded, "I was everything he'd let me be." She reached down and lifted the hem of her short skirt. Where the stocking tops ended, the tattoos began. They seemed to be in the same style as her dead boss's although newer.

"Did it hurt to have it done?" Fong asked.

"What do you think?" she said blowing a line of smoke past Fong's left ear.

He began to answer but sensed her retreating. He moved to the cop standing guard at the bar-room door. "Don't let her leave." Fong took out his wallet and handed over several bills. "Buy her a drink if she needs one, but she's to stay here until I come back."

Back in Bob's office, Li Chou, the plump head of CSU was finishing his work. Fong had already crossed swords with this man during the investigation into the abortion clinic bombings that eventually led to the killing of Angel Michael. "But that was then and this is now," Fong thought.

"Anything, Li Chou?" Fong asked.

The man looked up from his work and stared at Fong as if he didn't initially recognize him. Then something that could pass for a smile crossed his face, "Not yet."

No "sir" on the end of the sentence Fong noted. Well, he'd played the insubordination game himself often enough in the past so he let it pass. "Initial thoughts then, Li Chou?"

"Small calibre gun. Burn marks on the skin inside his left ear suggests that he put the gun in there . . . then put a teensy hole through his stupid head." Two of Li Chou's assistants giggled.

Fong's responding silence killed the hilarity in the room. Li Chou smiled and prompted his guys with, "Teensy-weensy hole, I'd say." Laughter, although somewhat forced, greeted Li

Chou's comment. Fong looked at the CSU guys. They were much closer to Li Chou's age than his. Li Chou was their dim sum ticket, not him. Fong nodded then cut through the tittering saying, "Are you right-handed, Li Chou?"

"Yeah, so?"

"So pretend that the stapler on the desk is a gun, okay?"

"Sure," Li Chou said slowly as he made a funny face for his guys. "Funny kinda gun, wouldn't you say?"

"So sit in the chair over there," Fong said. Li Chou made yet another face then did as Fong asked. "Now grip the stapler as if it were a gun. You're right-handed so use your right hand. Good. Now put it in your left ear."

The man tried to do it then realized that he couldn't get his finger to the trigger and still keep the gun in his ear. A look of real hatred crossed the man's face. "So what?" Li Chou demanded.

"So Mr. Clayton was right-handed too. That's so what," Fong spat back.

Too late, Fong realized that he had embarrassed Li Chou in front of his subordinates. Fong glanced over and the younger men made themselves look as busy as they could. Fong knew he should apologize. He knew that losing face was a real thing in this world but he couldn't resist adding, "If your English was better, you would have seen that from his writing."

Of course, if Fong hadn't been so cocky he would have bothered to read the dead man's final words on the notepad. It would not be until almost eighteen months later, in a far-off Western Canadian town called Kananaskis, that he would finally get a hint of what the International Exchange Institute actually exchanged.

Back at his office on the Bund, Fong was greeted by the head of the business section of Special Investigations. The man was a few years older than Fong and had at one time run a major corporation in Hong Kong. Run it just a tad on the wrong side of the law. When Hong Kong came back to the fold of Mother China, the man was offered two options: either join Special Investigations and work for the good of China or spend his remaining days in Ti Lan Chou, the world's largest political prison. The man moved his family to Shanghai and began to work for Special Investigations. And in many ways he was happier than he'd ever been. He drove a more modest car, he no longer spent time in expensive Japanese teahouses and he had actually relearned to appreciate his wife, which was helped along by his inability to finance his mistress. Kenneth Lo was now an elegant man in a somewhat pedestrian world.

He insisted on being called, like many Chinese from Hong Kong, by his British name. Fong could put up with that because Kenneth Lo was a talented forensic accountant and his computer skills were second only to Chen's in the office. Fong pointed to the chair across the desk from him. Kenneth sat and opened a large folder.

"So, Kenneth, what did the International Exchange Institute do to make cash?" Fong asked in English.

"It's hard to tell."

That surprised Fong. "Any ideas?"

"Some, but nothing sound. It seems to have something to do with Anhui Province."

"What could they want from that backwater?"

"I can't tell you 'til I get further into the computer's hard drive. But there's a problem."

"What a surprise – a problem with technology, who would have guessed?"

"Do you want to hear the problem, Detective Zhong, or are you content with making nasty remarks about the twentieth century's most important technological advance?"

Fong took a breath and bridged his delicate fingers in front of his face, "Tell me the problem."

"The man's hard drive has a series of complex locking mechanisms on it. I'm worried that if I go at the locks too quickly, I could trigger booby traps that would erase the material we need on it."

Fong thought about that but didn't speak.

Kenneth shifted positions in his chair. "Can we attack this another way?"

"How?" Fong asked.

"Just how important is the man's business activities to his death? What I mean to say is, do the events of Mr. Clayton's work necessarily intersect with the fact of his demise? I mean, aren't there compartments, yes, that's what I mean, aren't there compartments – I like that phrase – compartments in which we keep the separate sections of our lives? So it is possible, isn't it, that in one compartment Mr. Clayton had his work? And in another he had the part of his life that induced his death? Isn't that a possibility? In fact, why does what the company did have anything to do with Mr. Clayton's demise?"

Fong wanted to say because it probably does but thought of the girl in the bar and said, "You may be right."

"Then why not let me go at the guy's hard drive the safe way. Slow is safe in this case."

Fong thought about that then said, "Okay."

Kenneth gathered together his papers and stood. At the door he stopped and said, "It could take a while."

Fong wasn't pleased. "When you're done, will I have full access to that material on Mr. Clayton's computer?"

Kenneth nodded. As he left the office, he passed by the commissioner, who was cutting a path in the carpet to Fong's office. Fong sensed this approach before he actually saw him and grabbed his phone, hit a number on his speed dial before his doorway filled with the angry backlit figure of the commissioner – the man who had personally appointed Li Chou as the new head of CSU.

To Fong's surprise, Lily's voice came on the phone. *"Dui!"* Fong had hit her number on the speed dial by mistake. "Who fucked this?" Lily said in her own peculiar variant of the English language. "Who fucked this?" she repeated.

For a heartbeat, Fong wanted to correct his ex-wife's English slang. Fortunately he decided against it, hung up and turned to another point of wrath in his life, the commissioner of police for the Shanghai district.

Late that night, a little less well for the pasting he'd taken from the commissioner, Fong returned to the bar. The police officer was still at the door. The secretary was still at the bar. She was very drunk. Under his breath, Fong said to the man, "You have any change for me?"

"In this place? Are you kidding, sir? Luckily, she has a credit card."

Fong nodded and approached the lady who was swaying to the music that came from the speakers over the bar.

He sat beside her. The alcohol made her sweat and induced her perfume to release its scent. Fong turned to her but before he could open his mouth she spoke to his image in the mirror behind the bar, "You ever been in love, Detective?"

Fong was so surprised by the question that he almost answered, "I loved my first wife more than the air that sustains my being," but caught himself and said simply, "Yes."

She looked more closely at his image in the mirror. "You have, haven't you?"

He nodded.

"He was a lot older than me."

"Bob?"

She nodded. "He was going to marry me." She wagged an elegant finger at her drunken self in the mirror and corrected herself. "He *told* me he was going to marry me." Without warning, her control abandoned her and she yelled, "He promised me!" and threw her highball glass at her image in the mirror. The sound of the crashing shards of glass was drowned out by her screaming. Then there was an unnatural silence. As if the world held its breath. Then quiet words tumbled from her lips and her tears fell on the bar and Fong almost reached over to comfort her.

But he didn't. Instead he arrested her for the murder of her boss, whom she loved, who had promised to marry her.

He didn't get back to his rooms on the grounds of the Shanghai Theatre Academy until almost three in the morning. Usually he entered from the west gate and went directly home. But that night, the tears of the woman he'd arrested for killing the man she loved seemed to have opened a wide hole inside him. The image of her crying at the bar wouldn't go quietly into his mind's storage vault. Instead it grabbed the sides and fought. Screamed and shrieked and refused to go into the darkness. So he walked the long way around and entered the far gate. The heat of the day had finally abated a few hours back and the scent of the sea tinged the gentle easterly wind.

Fong's city was quiet. Shanghai was never fully asleep but it got quiet from 2:30 to 5:30 in the morning when the 18 million souls finally allowed today to become yesterday. Fu Tsong had loved this time – after today, before tomorrow.

A moment of vertigo passed through him. He leaned against the cool mud wall of the nearest building to stop the world from spinning – if only for a moment – and felt as alone as he'd ever been since he cast his wife's body into the quick-drying cement of the huge construction pit deep in the Pudong, almost seven years ago. He shook that thought from his head and stood up straight. He was getting too old for late nights – and young love. Looking over his shoulder, he realized he was leaning against one of the old theatre's side doors. Naturally it would be the theatre. The poster to his right announced that the place was playing Geoff Hyland's production of *Hamlet*. Fong noticed that the poster art was better than usual. Then he noted that the fabulous Hao Yong was playing Gertrude – "Was she already old enough to play Hamlet's mother?" he wondered. Fong still remembered her incredible performance as the young Indian girl in Geoff's first production in Shanghai, *The Ecstasy of Rita Joe*. And now she was playing the melancholy prince's mom. Fong nodded and said to the air, "I guess she is."

Fong remembered the rehearsal he had sat in on two weeks earlier and Geoff's hand on his shoulder. And the business card with the plea. Nonsense. Just more Western paranoia about working in the Middle Kingdom.

Fong reached into his pocket and felt the key to the theatre on his key ring. He remembered the night Fu Tsong had given it to him. Images raced through his mind. Fu Tsong's face became Hao Yong's and that became the face of the woman-who-killed-the-man-she-loved.

When he finally found sleep that night, he dreamt of women's tears falling and him trying to catch them before they disappeared into the dense richness of the Chinese earth.

CHAPTER FOUR

A DEATH, A MEMORY AND A NOTE

The next day was about paperwork. Not Fong's favourite thing, although he was pleased to be able to pawn some of it off on Shrug and Knock. That night Fong picked up his toddler daughter Xiao Ming at Lily and Chen's rooms as he did every Wednesday. They had dinner outside on Good Food Street, surrounded by the savoury smells of the cooking mixed with the human smell of thousands of people and the gentle hint of Yangtze's saltwater tang on the evening breeze. Xiao Ming sat on Fong's lap as they ate. Her dexterity was incredible and she would try anything Fong ordered. As the waitress cleared the last dish, Xiao Ming let loose with a really loud belch. Many other diners looked at her. Several applauded. A smile crinkled her face followed by a rolling laugh that came all the way from her belly. Fong threw his arms around her and gave her a big hug.

She responded by grabbing his arms in her little hands and whispering, "Daddy."

They hustled through the throngs on Good Food Street and Fong hailed a cab. He had managed to get two tickets to the theatre for them. Xiao Ming was enchanted by the whirling, dancing, juggling, singing thing that was Peking Opera. It gratified Fong, who had always loved it.

They fought their way through the crowd and took their seats near the front of the balcony. As soon as the lights went down, Xiao Ming climbed up on his lap. As the performance unfolded, he explained the magic of what was taking place. "When she carries the stick with the tassels it indicates that she is riding a horse. See how her posture changes as well and her gait. As if she is being carried, as if she no longer has her feet on the ground." Xiao Ming smiled and imitated the posture while still on his lap. The scene ended as cymbals crashed and the actress struck a stunning pose on one foot. Xiao Ming clapped her small hands and shrieked "*Hao*" along with the rest of the crowd. As the performance proceeded, she held her father's hand tight, eyes bright with excitement. And he watched her. Fell into her eyes. Remembered his own joy. How odd it was. The one thing he regretted was that his first wife would never meet his child. How odd.

Another loud clash of cymbals brought him back to the theatre. The lead actor struck a pose, lifted a foot parallel to the ground then reached up and pulled the feather on his headdress down into his mouth. The horns sounded. The actor shrieked. The crowd "*Hao*'ed" until they were hoarse.

Fong explained the meaning of the juggling and dances to her, just as his father had explained them to him. Then he added new ideas that his father wouldn't even begin to understand. "This is something that is of us, Xiao Ming. It's not like McDonald's or computers that come from faraway. We must keep alive such things as this." She nodded then turned her eyes back to the stage, to the stylized miracle that is Peking Opera.

Six hours later, the phone on Fong's night table awoke him from a deep sleep. It took Fong a few short moments to understand that the terrified voice he heard belonged to the janitor of the academy's theatre. It took a few longer moments for Fong to pull on his clothing and race over to the old theatre. But it took many, many, much longer moments before Fong could believe the information his eyes were sending to his brain.

A body – sirens in the distance – at the end of a rope – sirens louder – dangling from the ceiling or the flies or whatever theatre people called them. Still swinging. Perhaps the earth was in motion. Something important was falling into the caverns of Fong's troubled heart. His enemy, his rival, the Canadian theatre director Geoff Hyland was no more.

"Something ends but something else always begins," an old voice whispered inside Fong's head.

The doors of the theatre crashed open. Police officers. Something infinitely profane in a sometimes sacred place.

"Sir?" Fong had forgotten that he had called Captain Chen before he ran to the theatre. Forgotten that this was a crime scene. "You knew him, didn't you sir?"

Fong remembered the weight of Geoff's hand on his shoulder and the writing on the back of a business card – which he had ignored out of anger, folly – jealousy. Fong's wife had died on an abortionist's table carrying a child that could well have been fathered by this man, by Geoffrey Hyland.

"Yes. He was my first wife's lover."

Fong didn't wait for an answer. What answer could poor Chen give? As Fong climbed the stairs to the stage to take a closer look, a voice from the darkness stopped him, "Stay off that. This is a crime site. And this time at least we are going to follow procedures." It was Li Chou, the head of Crime Scene Unit. He didn't wait for Fong's response. He waved a fleshy paw and his team of six technicians hopped up on the stage. They taped off the area, set up harsh arc lights and began their work. Fong felt like a child looking in a store window at a toy he knew he'd never be able to touch. Suddenly Li Chou was right there in front of him, on the other side, the right side, of the tape. "You stay there. Don't even think about coming across."

The man's voice was unnaturally loud. For a brief moment Fong wondered why, then he got it. Fong's subordinates were there. He had embarrassed Li Chou in front of his people and now Li Chou was returning the favour.

"You!" Li Chou shouted to Captain Chen. "I want a word with you." Chen waited for Fong's approval. Fong nodded and Captain Chen moved toward Li Chou. As he passed, Fong whispered, "Tell him whatever he wants to know." Chen stopped. Fong said it again with stronger emphasis, "Whatever he wants. It's time for you to deal with the politics of the department if you want to stay with Special Investigations. You're married now; think about that sometimes. Now tell him whatever he wants."

Captain Chen gave Fong an odd look then ducked beneath the tape and hopped up on the stage. Fong retreated to the back of the theatre, where only two weeks ago he had sat with the man who was now swinging gently from the rafters of the stage. A man who had left a business card beneath his collar, on the back of which were the words *Help me, Fong*.

Captain Chen disappeared into the wings of the theatre with Li Chou as the CSU technicians meticulously laid out a grid on the stage floor with string. It always seemed to come back to this. To a theatre. To the darkness – and of course to his first wife, the actress Fu Tsong, whose image seemed to emerge from the seats, from the smells, from the very darkling light of this place.

This stage on the campus of the Shanghai Theatre Academy had been his wife's favourite theatre though she had performed all over Asia. Its seats were a wreck. Its lighting system was so archaic that it tripped breakers all over the neighbourhood almost every time they turned it on. Its damp mustiness was so intense it entered your mouth and nose, tainted any food or drink you brought in with you, and left a marked odour on the clothes you wore. It was inescapable. So was this place's history. "That's what makes a theatre a place of ghosts, dear Fong," her sweet voice whispered beside him in the dark. It was a voice he knew so very well. He was going to turn to her but he knew she wasn't there. Dead people were dead. They did not whisper sweetly in the darkness or hold hands or soothe the yearning of the heart.

He had sat in the exact same seat two weeks before, the ghost of Fu Tsong beside him. Geoffrey Hyland, his wife's lover, had been on the stage. "Naturally, in a place like this he'd be directing *Hamlet*. It's a play about ghosts," Fong had whispered to the darkness.

Geoffrey's elegant frame had moved across the stage, his homely translator at his side. For the briefest moment, Geoff stopped as if suspended in space then he was on his frenetic way again. Opening night was only two days away and Geoffrey was jumpier than Fong had ever seen him. He called over the actor playing Rosencrantz and loudly asked for the satchel he carried. The young actor gave the large leather thing over to Geoff, who thanked him, then yelled some instruction in his childish Mandarin all the way to the other side of the stage. His translator quickly corrected his Mandarin without Geoff knowing it and she warned all those within earshot to watch their manners when it came to criticizing Geoff. It struck Fong that the woman was quite protective of Geoff. It made him smile. Then wince.

Geoff called the fight director onstage and spoke to him in a whisper. The fight director called the actors playing Hamlet and Laertes, who entered from stage left. Geoff nodded then headed off into the wings. The fight director set the two actors in their starting positions then dropped a handkerchief. When it hit the stage, the two drew their swords and Laertes lunged at Hamlet. Fong didn't know this fight director, but he was immediately concerned because the actor playing Laertes seemed to be all anger and little skill. His lunges at Hamlet seemed truly intent upon hurting the other actor. The fight director stepped in just as Laertes seemed about to take a swing at Hamlet's head.

Geoff returned from the stage-right wings and flipped the large satchel to Guildenstern saying, "Give this to your better half."

"It contains the letter, sir?" asked Guildenstern.

"Indeed it does. The death letter!" Geoff said in his best booga-booga voice. Guildenstern moved offstage with the satchel, then Geoff turned to the actors playing Hamlet and Laertes, "Fight fixed, boys?"

Hamlet gave a nod but the actor playing Laertes glowered and stomped off. "What's his beef?" asked the fight director.

Before his plain-faced translator could interject, Geoff responded in his ghastly Mandarin, "I broke his rice bowl, I guess" or it could have been "dog go bowl puke" – it was hard to tell since Geoff completely ignored the tones of the words. He had the sounds right, but without the tones who could tell what he was trying to say? The translator quickly clarified Geoff's meaning while the fight director laughed out loud. The translator glowered him into silence.

Geoff, oblivious to all the linguistic comings and goings, moved gracefully across the stage touching a set piece here, giving a word to an actor there, and finally turned toward the auditorium.

He stopped – as if in mid-air, again.

The assuredness that gave him such elegance evaporated and he reverted to being the fifty-year-old man that he was. He put a hand up to his eyes to shield them from the stage light and stared out into the darkness.

"Could he see me?" Fong wondered. He didn't know, but it made him squirm. This man had known his deceased wife in a way that he had not, on a plane to which Fong could not ascend. They had met on the field of art and created something that endured for many years in the minds of all who had seen it.

"Who's there?" Geoffrey's voice was raspier than Fong remembered. Then something struck Fong.

"Isn't that the opening line of this silly play?" Fong called back from the darkness.

"Fuck me with a stick!"

It took Fong a moment to translate that, although he couldn't begin to guess what it meant.

"What is your sorry ass doing here?" Geoff called out.

That Fong got, but he was surprised. Was it possible that Geoffrey Hyland was happy to see him?

"I repeat, what is your sorry ass doing here?"

"Haunting you, I guess."

"Well, you got the right play for it." Geoffrey turned to the actors and then called out into the house, "Let's start at the top." Geoff hopped off the stage followed at a respectful distance by his translator. Fong wondered why the phrase "at a respectful distance" had such a strong whiff of the hated phrase "no dogs or Chinese" which was common parlance in much of Shanghai before the liberation. He looked at the woman.

In the Chinese theatre, where female beauty was everywhere, this middle-aged woman stood out for her profound blandness. Her features were hard to describe. Plain was the wrong word for them. Homely was better. He looked more closely at the woman. He'd seen, and to be honest, ignored her for years. Although she gave her name to foreigners as Deborah Tong, she actually had the unlikely name of Da Wei. She'd been Geoff's translator since the first time Geoff directed in Shanghai almost ten years ago. Fong had traded only a few words with Da Wei over all those years. Her English was perfect and up to date with all the colloquialisms that drive any new English speaker mad. She also, apparently, had a good working knowledge of the theatre – an essential for anyone translating for Geoff. No doubt she had to deal with the ostracism ladled out by Chinese to one of their own who dealt with Westerners, but it didn't seem to weigh heavily on her. But that's all Fong knew about her – not where she came from, not where on the academy's campus she lived, not even her marital status – although at her age he assumed she'd be married – not even where or how she learned her English.

Geoff headed toward Fong. The translator stayed "at a respectful distance" from both of them. Fong made a mental note to check on Da Wei's background then promptly forgot it when Geoff took the seat directly behind him. The work lights dimmed, but just before they were completely out Fong noticed a young Chinese man in a suit slip off the stage and follow Geoff and another, older, man rise from his seat near the stage and move back toward them.

A lengthy silence followed. Then a simple table lamp sitting on the floor near the edge of the stage came on. The dim light revealed a raised roughly hewn wooden platform that was slanted toward the audience. On it was a near-naked figure, face down – screaming. A single violin note came from the back of the auditorium. The figure turned toward it – toward the audience, toward us – and began to silently plead: No, no, please no.

Dark figures approached. One put his hand over the man's mouth while the other two dressed him – dressed him for his job – to lead us through the dark alleyways of Hamlet's heart.

"He dies for us every night," said Geoff from the darkness. Something slithered up Fong's spine. "Like Prometheus. Those with special gifts must suffer for our edification. It has always been thus." Then as if conducting he said, "And in just a moment . . . "

The stage lights shifted, taking the anguished man from sight and exposing a small man in a large ratty overcoat and hard-soled shoes shaking from the cold and trying not to drop his rather large spear.

"Spear's a bit long for him, isn't it?" asked Fong.

"I don't use props very much, you may have noticed, Fong. Only when they are the quickest way to reveal the truth. Otherwise I find them a clunky nuisance."

Fong thought about that. Yes, in all of Geoff's productions there were, in fact, very few props or sets.

"It's night, Fong. And Elsinore Castle has been under assault from the Poles for almost a decade. It's the fourteenth century . . . "

" . . . and I assume no one could attack at night in the fourteenth century," Fong said, completing Geoff's thought. He turned to Geoff and saw close behind him the young man he had seen slide off the stage and the older man who had been sitting down front. Both were clearly Beijing men. Was Geoff now deemed worthy of having keepers by the powers up north? But why would a theatre director need a keeper? Let alone two?

"That being the case," Geoffrey prompted, "the king wouldn't waste the time of real soldiers to guard the walls so he'd . . . "

" . . . enlist the clerk and the night-soil collector."

"Very good, Fong. I think of them as the tinker and the tailor myself," Geoffrey said, indicating the small man onstage who stood very still for a moment then whirled around. His large spear dropped to the ground with a clang. He fell to his hands and knees trying to find it in the darkness but couldn't. Then, as if he heard something, he rose slowly and peered out into the darkness. Geoff leaned in close to Fong and said, "And here it comes . . . "

"Who's there?" the poor man whispers.

"As I said, the first line of the play."

"So you do know your Shakespeare, Fong."

"Thanks to Fu Tsong." The moment he said it he realized it was the very first time he had ever spoken his wife's name in her lover's company. It was as if he'd allowed two separate parts of himself to bleed together. It was as if he'd moved to the other side of a mirror where his image lived.

From the depths of the stage darkness the new watch comes to replace the old. With them is a nobleman, Horatio. The man questions the guard about the sightings of the ghost. Fong immediately liked the young man playing Horatio. Modest, honest and straightforward. But he didn't like his insights:

"In the most high and palmy state of Rome, A little ere the mightiest Julius fell, The graves stood tenantless and the sheeted dead Did squeak and gibber in the Roman streets: As stars with trains of fire and dews of blood, Disasters in the sun; and the moist star Upon whose influence Neptune's empire stands Was sick almost to dooms-day with eclipse . . . "

"If only evil were mirrored by a cantankerousness in nature, my job would be easier," Fong thought. But he'd often found the reverse. A sadistic father's savagery could as easily take place on a beautiful spring day when the cherry blossoms are scenting the city as in the midst of a torrential sky letting.

The new guards, Marcellus and Bernardo, lead Horatio to the place they last saw the ghost. Horatio sees nothing and is about to leave when he senses something and turns. That single violin note again from the back of the auditorium. There is nothing there that we can see but clearly Horatio sees something. He staggers back.

"The darkness speaks to him," Geoffrey says into Fong's ear.

Fong thought about that. Darkness can most assuredly speak.

Hamlet makes his first entrance. The light strikes the man's face and for a fleeting instant he looks oddly like a younger Asian version of Geoff. Fong's breath catches in his throat. Then the violin note again and he too is addressed by the darkness. This time we hear the darkness speak too. The voice comes from somewhere high in the rafters of the old building.

Geoff's staging was spare, almost entirely devoid of props. Only the most essential elements were used, but it had a real elegance – a grace that was present in all of Geoff's work.

The dreadful message of murder by a brother is delivered and received. But the ambiguity of Geoff's staging leaves it unclear as to the nature of this message. Is it honest? A message from the darkness that your uncle killed your father and that you are to avenge the murder. Hard to swallow in the light of day let alone in a voice from the darkness. Fong played with the phrase *voice from the darkness* for a moment. It reminded him of something. Finally he asked, "Is 'a voice from the darkness' from your Bible?"

"I'm not sure. I know there is a voice from a burning bush."

Fong turned around to look at Geoffrey. "From a bush?"

"From a burning bush, actually."

"Was it important what the bush said?"

"Well, it was God speaking . . . "

"From a bush? A hedge? Not even a tree or the sky? What god would choose to talk from a shrubbery? Surely no one of any importance bothered to obey this voice."

"No one important, just Moses, patriarch of Jews, Christians and Muslims."

"That explains a lot."

"Really?"

"Sure. Jews, Christians and Muslims have lots of problems. Maybe they stem, excuse the pun, from listening to bushes."

Geoffrey laughed.

Fong had never heard him laugh before. Despite himself, he liked the sound. He didn't know what to do with that. When he looked up, Polonius's farewell to his son, Laertes, was taking place.

Fong listened to Polonius's advice to his son:

"Beware of entrance to a quarrel; but being in,

Beaer't that th' opposed may beware of thee.
Give every man thine ear, but few thy voice."

Fong turned to Geoff, "Why is this man thought of as a fool? His advice is sound."

"I agree, Fong. His outside may be foolish but he is no fool. Remember, he managed to keep his position under two different administrations. Not always an easy thing to do but something that I assume someone like yourself who works for a Communist dictatorship would be able to appreciate." Before Fong could protest, Geoff continued, "I think Polonius is stupid like a fox. In fact, I have him supplying the poison that Claudius puts in Hamlet senior's ear."

"Is that in the play?"

"It's implied if you follow the logic of the events."

Fong thought about that too. Events do have logic. They even sequence themselves. He had noticed of late that his life had an odd logic to it. Like a play in three acts. And here he was just finishing his second act, watching *Hamlet*. He finished his first act watching *Twelfth Night* with his first wife, Fu Tsong, playing Viola. That production had been directed by Geoffrey Hyland as well.

Geoffrey was still talking. Fong hadn't been listening but picked up just the very end of Geoffrey's statement: " . . . you have good eyes, Fong. You can see, really see." Geoff put a hand on Fong's shoulder by the collar of his summer-weight jacket. Fong couldn't believe he would do that but before he could protest, Geoff continued, "I don't know about in your work, Fong, but in mine something odd happens when you achieve a certain level of skill. Your life slips into your work. Not obvious. Not open. But absolutely there, for those with good eyes, to see. When I was in drama school, an entire lifetime ago, I assisted the single most talented director I'd ever seen work. He was my only teacher, Fong. He was the reason I went back to school. One rehearsal, he arrived late – really not like him – and he set right into working on a scene. He worked on it with incredible energy, almost frenzy. Then he ran it. When he finished, he turned to me and said, "So what d'you think?"

"Well, I was a student. Stupid. So I told him. 'It looks like a car crash.' His face sort of opened up and he began to laugh. 'What?' I asked. Then through his laughter he said, 'I just totalled my car on the way to rehearsal. That's why I was late.' It really wasn't until years later that I realized what was going on. He was so hooked up, so in touch with himself that everything he put onstage was a response to the reality of his life. I always wanted to get that close to myself. I worked at it, Fong, and now somehow it's happening. Everything important in my life is up there on that stage. Everything that's happening in my life is right there for anyone to see, so long as they have the right eyes, like yours, Fong."

Geoff removed his hand from Fong's shoulder. Fong turned to look at him. Then Fong saw two Caucasian women approaching them. One was small and pinched and clutched a red zippered binder to her chest. The other was tall, dark-haired, older and may have at one time been attractive in a coarse kind of way. Were these some sort of Western keepers? The older, taller woman stood back and brooded. She was the kind of person who leached light from a room. The smaller one strode forward as if she owned the place.

"My producers – I call them my Screaming me-me's," Geoff whispered.

"I think we need to work on the opening," said small Miss Pinch Face Me-me. "It's flaccid."

Fong looked to Geoff. Who was this woman? And the opening was anything but flaccid. It was pure liquid. Classic Geoff.

Geoff made a cursory introduction. "Kitty Pants, Inspector Zhong Fong, head of Special Investigations, Shanghai District."

"Hi," said Ms. Pants without any warmth or even really bothering to take in Fong.

Fong stood. He wasn't about to be dismissed by the likes of this sour woman.

"We have work to do, Mr. Fong."

"Inspector Zhong," Fong corrected her. She was clearly surprised that he spoke English.

"Yes, well, could you excuse us for a moment?" It wasn't really a question. "Come." She signalled for Geoff to follow her. Fong had met many theatre people during the time he had been with Fu Tsong. He could sense who was and who wasn't of that world. Geoff most assuredly was. Miss Pants certainly wasn't. So what was Geoff doing answering to this tight-assed little woman?

As Geoff moved up the aisle with Miss Pinch Face, the two Chinese watchers flanked them. What the fuck was going on here?

Fong shifted in his seat. Something fell from beneath the collar of his coat, where Geoff's hand had rested so uncomfortably. Fong eyed the business card that now lay on the floor. He noted the position of the watchers and when he thought it safe, leaned over as if to tie up his shoe and picked up the card. Under the italicized words *The Play's the Thing* were Geoff's name and contact numbers in both Mandarin and English. Fong turned the card over. There, in a scrawling hand, were slashed the words: *I have no right to ask, but help me, Fong.*

And now Geoffrey Hyland was no more. Fong sat back in his seat and thought about the card. The request for help – and how out of bitterness, and jealousy, he had ignored it.

Four hours later, Li Chou handed over the crime site to Fong with the pointing of a fat index finger and the warning that his people would be back to "pack it up" later. As he left the theatre, Li Chou said loudly to Fong, "Don't make a mess."

"I'll wash my hands and everything," Fong snarked back, but he felt small the moment the words were out of his mouth.

Once Li Chou and his men had left the theatre, Fong ducked under the tape and headed toward the stage.

He'd seldom ventured onto a stage. In fact the only time he remembered actually being on a stage was in an attempt to hide himself and an American woman, Amanda Pitman, in the days before his internal exile.

A stage was Fu Tsong's domain. Not his. His place in a theatre was in the darkness of the audience. Fu Tsong's place was in the light. She somehow seemed to bring the light.

He took a deep breath and let it out slowly, then hopped up on the stage.

The platforms were arranged like a shattered cross. Fong knew the basic Christian significance of this but it carried no resonance for him. He walked over to the body that still hung by its neck. It seemed to be in motion as if it were the bell at the bottom of a long pendulum. As Fong approached, an unwelcome thought flitted through his consciousness. "Fu Tsong had loved what this body encased."

He took a breath and then another. His heart was racing. He bent over from the waist. "Fuck, I'm going to faint," he thought. He yanked off his jacket, crumpled it and held it to his mouth. His breathing became less laboured. His heart stopped racing. Slowly he regained control. Then he turned back to the body.

Fong knew his men were watching him.

A young detective stepped forward. Fong held up his hand. The man stopped. Fong hoped that when he spoke his voice wouldn't wobble. "Get me the forensic report as soon as it's available." The young detective gave a curt bow and left through the side door by the pinrail.

Chen waited for him to issue more orders. He was careful to keep his eyes down. Finally he asked, "It's a suicide, isn't it, sir?"

It sure as hell looked like a suicide. The ladder Geoff had climbed and then kicked aside was lying where it ought to be forward and downstage from him. The knotted rope around his neck had the traditional look of a hangman's noose. "Was there a note?" Fong asked.

"No one has found one yet," said Chen.

"Get me access to his room. Was he staying at the theatre academy or in a hotel? He usually stayed on the grounds."

The cops looked at Fong. They all digested the information that Fong had known the deceased. More mystery for them about their boss. "I'll find out," said another young cop and headed out.

"Chen, photograph the scene, I'm more confident in your abilities than in Li Chou's." There was a chorus of muffled chuckles.

Fong turned to his men. "Enough. We have work to do." Turning to the nearest cop, he said, "Find me the stage manager. I want to know which actors were last to leave the theatre." Before anyone could question him, he added, "Find me another ladder." Then, to everyone's surprise, Fong turned and walked over to the stage-right proscenium arch. He pointed to a smudge mark of some sort on the pillar eight feet above the ground and said, "Take a photo of that too, will you Chen? And bag a sample."

"Sir?" Fong ignored Chen's question and marched across the stage to the other proscenium arch and looked at it carefully. "Is there something . . . ?"

"Later, Chen, later. Let's stand that ladder up now."

After carefully noting its position, marked by Li Chou's people on the stage floor, they righted the ladder. Fong looked up at the hanging body then allowed his eyes to follow the noose. The rope went up to a pulley attached to a wooden batten dead hung from the ceiling by thick chains. The rope then continued from the pulley offstage until it met another larger pulley then headed down to the floor stage left, where it was tied off to a pinrail. Fong headed over to the pinrail. He reached out and held the rope. Its thick tautness was not pleasing. He gave it a yank. Immediately yelps came from the stage as the body twitched. Fong ignored them and looked around. Chen pointed toward a set of iron weights attached to the pinrail. "Counterweights, sir, to make it easy to lift a dead weight. Sorry, sir, no offence intended."

Fong looked at Chen. "None taken. Thanks." But Fong wasn't really paying attention. He was trying to recall a story Fu Tsong had told him about counterweights. Something about Christ and counterweights. Fong shook his head. That couldn't be right – Christ and counterweights? He sat heavily in the chair that was by the pinrail. Then he stood and looked at the chair. A simple school chair. He looked up and down the wings. It was the only chair there. He looked at it a second time then strode back onstage and climbed the ladder to Geoff.

It was only later, when Fong recalled Fu Tsong's story, that he realized he hadn't noted a crucial fact: how much counter-weight was on the line.

Face-to-face with Geoff, everything else receded into a misted background – the theatre, his cops, Captain Chen – as if in a film when the camera zooms in tight. Here, with death, Fong was at the apex, in the very centre. In focus.

He snapped on a pair of latex gloves and touched Geoff's face.

The flesh was almost hard to the touch. Already dense, spongy. The blood had, upon death, pooled in the lower extremities of his body leaving a tough plastic-like consistency to the skin. But beneath the skin, Fong knew that rot was setting in quickly. Nothing dead resisted rot long in Shanghai's summer heat. Fong leaned in to look at the rope marks. There was a lot of ligature burn up and down the neck. Fong hoped Geoff's neck had snapped. The image of Geoff strangling slowly on the end of the rope was not pleasing – Fong had seen hangings that didn't go off well, the phrase "without a hitch" came to him but he put it aside. If it's not done right it can take several terrifying minutes before a man suffocates at the end of a rope. A scent caught Fong's attention. He couldn't identify it but it was not a body odour.

Captain Chen had set up the other ladder and was climbing up to take pictures of Geoff.

Fong waited until Chen was at body level then pointed to the neck. "Shoot this."

Chen did, then asked, "Is there something I'm not seeing? Those marks are to be expected in a suicide, aren't they?"

"Maybe," Fong said and descended a rung to get a better look at Geoff's fingers. Long. Tapered. He bent the wrist to look beneath the fingernails.

Chen took another picture then asked, "Scrapings?"

Fong shook his head and descended.

"I don't see any defensive markings, sir. Do you?"

On the stage floor, he stepped back and looked at the body again. Trying to get a fuller picture. "I want the body to go to Lily first. I want a full toxicology report." Chen nodded. Then Fong remembered the odour. He raced quickly up the ladder.

"What?" said Chen surprised.

"Hold him still."

Chen did and Fong pulled aside Geoff's jacket. He was wearing a vest. Odd for a hot day. On the inside pocket of the vest Fong found them.

"Flowers, sir?"

Fong took a deep breath of the fragrance. "Yes. Three different types of flowers."

"Tell Lily I want these identified." Fong said then as Chen descended his ladder Fong added, "and get me a Shakespeare expert too." Before Chen could ask why, Fong turned his attention back to Geoff.

It was only then that Fong noticed a slight paint stain on the outside of Geoff's right shoe.

From the back of the auditorium two men in suits, the Beijing men, watched and smiled. The older of the two took out a cell phone, punched in a speed-dial number and gave an order. Then he turned to the younger man. "You agree?"

The younger man smiled, "I do."

CHAPTER FIVE

GEOFF'S ROOM

ong was surprised. No. Shocked. Geoff's room was untouched – no quadrant markings, no gummy residue from print dusting, no drawers opened, no bed turned over, no floorboards lifted. Here it was maybe twenty-four hours after Geoff's death and the man's room had not been scoured by the Crime Scene Unit, fuck, it hadn't even been entered. Why? He stepped out of the room and closed the door. Then he turned to Chen. "Get Li Chou on your cell."

Chen began to ask why but found himself looking at Fong's retreating back. He punched in the CSU number on his cell phone and after a brief nastiness Li Chou consented to pick up. "Li Chou's on the line, sir," Chen called to Fong. Fong didn't turn. He seemed entranced by the pattern of the carpet in the guesthouse's corridor. Without looking up, Fong said, "Ask him why CSU hasn't been to Mr. Hyland's room."

Chen relayed the question then had to hold the phone away from his ear as Li Chou shouted his response then hung up.

Fong lifted his head, "So?"

"He says that he was denied access to the room."

"Who denied him access?"

"He says you did."

Fong thought about that for a moment. He certainly would

have liked to deny Li Chou access to the crime site, but after the unpleasantness in front of the men in the theatre even he wouldn't venture into that territory. "He claims he was denied access to the room?"

"Yes, sir."

Fong returned his attention to the complex pattern in the corridor carpet. He allowed his eye to trace one long wine red line as it intertwined with squares and circles of various colours and patterns and then disappeared beneath an intricate design of triangles and cubes. Several yards farther down the corridor he saw his wine red line emerge from the mess. He looked up.

"Did you deny Li Chou access to Mr. Hyland's room, Captain Chen?" Before the stunned man could answer, Fong held up his hand, "Just a joke, Captain Chen." Chen was visibly relieved.

"But someone did. I wonder who." What he did not add was the important part of the thought: "Why had CSU been denied access?" He turned away from Chen again and once more traced the wine red line in the carpet. His thoughts cascaded quickly: "Question: What is the result of denying CSU access to Geoff's room? Answer: It allows me to get in there first. Question: Who would want me to investigate a site before CSU? Answer: Someone who wanted a better chance of finding anything there was to find in Geoff's room and therefore what happened to Geoff in the theatre." No, that wasn't completely right. Fong stopped moving. But before he could figure out exactly what part of the thought was wrong, the image of the two Beijing politicos who had been Geoff's keepers popped into his head. Fong's breath caught in his throat.

Federal officers, Beijing politicos in Shanghai, no doubt with an agenda. They were the only ones powerful enough to block Li Chou from getting into Geoff's room. They may have already been in the room but were unable to find what they wanted. Fong thought about that then dismissed it. But for sure something that Geoff had been hiding is important to them. And they want him to find it and no doubt hand it over to them so they can figure out exactly what happened to Geoff. Again, he sensed a false assumption in his thinking but couldn't put his finger on it.

He turned to Chen. "Yellow-tape this. It's potentially a crime site."

"Aren't we going in?"

"Not yet. Somewhere to go first, we'll be back."

On his way out, Fong noticed that the key lady was different than the one he and Chen had seen on the way in. Key ladies, remnants of the old Communist control system, refused to allow visitors to have the room keys. Westerners always complained about this because they'd return to their guesthouses and have to search out the key lady to get into their own rooms – a process that could take up to an hour. Most places that foreigners frequented had scrapped this practice, but because the old campus where Geoff stayed was technically a working commune, the system was still in place. "Where's the lady who was here when we arrived?" Fong asked.

The key lady clearly didn't understand him.

Before Fong could launch into his favourite tirade about the advancement of incompetent party members, most often from the country, over native Shanghanese, Chen tried the question in a country accent and the woman responded, "We're covering for each other. We're always short. Don't know where they go. People just come and go as they please. I don't even know most of their names. It's hard to get good help these days." That certainly was the truth. Try to get anyone to do a menial job and you're lucky to keep him or her for even a few weeks. Fong thought of it as nothing more than another one of Shanghai's growing pains on its road to becoming one of the world's most powerful cities.

Outside the guesthouse, Fong consulted his private phone-book and dialled the number of the head of the Communist Party in Shanghai. The great man picked up on the third ring. That surprised Fong but he collected himself and requested access to the two Beijing keepers. The man heard Fong out and then, with barely concealed glee, gave him the phone number for Ti Lan Chou Prison.

The prison official took ten minutes to set up a meeting – at the prison of course.

Fong arrived on time at the prison, but naturally they made him wait. Fong knew they would. Despite that, he couldn't sit still. He was inundated with memories of his confinement here. That time had left deep slash cuts in his mind, deeper than he cared to acknowledge. It had taken a tremendous act of courage to force himself first to contact this place and then to walk through its tall iron doors. But there was nowhere else in Shanghai to contact the federal police force except here in Ti Lan Chou, the largest political prison in the world and a place where Fong had spent just under two of the hardest years of his life.

A door slammed in a far-off corridor. Fong flinched. He'd forgotten how loud prisons were. How noise bounced off the concrete and steel and bounded and bounded unhindered and undiminished by anything soft to soak it up.

Another sound, this of a key turning in a heavy lock fol-lowed closely by an electronic connection being made and the snapping-to of metal. Then the door opened. It was only then Fong realized that when the warden had left him alone in this room with the door closed and locked that he was not sure it would ever open again.

The two Beijing men entered. Fong thought to rise but decided against it.

Bad idea.

"Stand up, Traitor Zhong," said the older of the two.

Getting to his feet, Fong said, "I am the head of Special Investigations, Shanghai District . . . "

"You are as long as we let you be . . . Traitor Zhong."

Fong breathed in that truth then jumped quickly to the corollary. If they let me it's because I can do something of value for them. And what is that something?

The younger man lit a cigarette and said as if to no one in particular and as if apropos of nothing, "No one is above being replaced in the People's Republic of China. No one is that special." His pronunciation of the word *special* was particularly venomous. But Fong declined to take the bait and the invective splatted to the table like a dollop of glutinous brown sauce from a dish of Hei Pei pork.

The older man said, "Would you like to see the cell you spent two years in, Traitor Zhong? It's fortuitously available at this time."

Fong took a deep breath, "What do you want?"

"We want you to investigate the unfortunate passing of Mr. Hyland. What else would we want?" The man smiled. His teeth stuck out of his gums at odd angles, like fenceposts after a monsoon. "We expect your best efforts. We expect you to think creatively. We also expect something else."

"And that would be . . . ?"

"Your discretion, Traitor Zhong. You see, there could be much more here than may at first strike the eye."

Fong thought of the lines Hamlet says to Horatio about there being more things in heaven and earth than are ever dreamt of in philosophy. Then he got angry. "Why don't you just tell me what you know?"

The younger man smiled. "Maybe we don't know anything."

Fong almost snarked back "That would be no surprise," but he resisted that temptation. "Why were you assigned to keep an eye on Mr. Hyland?"

"He's a foreigner."

"He's been here before and I never saw keepers with him then."

"Maybe this time he had more on his mind than directing plays and fucking your wife."

Fong couldn't believe they'd gone there. All he could manage was, "What more?"

The older man leaned against the wall, "Two weeks ago, Mr. Hyland entered the Jade Buddha Temple at 7:15 a.m. Once inside, he managed to lose our surveillance team in the morning crowd. He was gone for a day and a half. We don't know where he went or what he did." The man shifted position. "We want to know."

"What do you suspect?"

The man pushed off the wall and began to pace with an oddly rhythmic elegance. "Mr. Hyland was a lonely man. A sentimental man. Someone who perhaps was looking for something to which he could dedicate the final years of his life."

"He was an artist. Artists have their art. They seldom need more."

"We think Mr. Hyland needed more," shot back the younger man.

The older man tossed a grainy photo onto the table. A young, handsome Han Chinese man in Western casual dress was hopping into a taxicab in some downtown area. There was a Caucasian in the back seat.

Fong took the photo, "Shanghai?"

"Yes. Near Julu Lu and Nanjing Lu."

"When?"

"Over three months ago."

"And I'm supposed to know who this is?"

"No. You're not. The important thing is the man in the back seat of the cab. He's Mr. Geoffrey Hyland."

"Geoffrey was here three months ago?"

"Without papers."

"So this wasn't a suicide, then?"

The older man looked at the younger man who looked at Fong. "I don't think either of us said or implied that, did we?" He looked to the older man who shook his head.

"We didn't," said the older politico. "Keep in touch, Traitor Zhong. Now, I think both you and we have other things to do with our day." He made an odd hand motion that was meant to be dismissive but came off more as the appropriate gesture for someone who says goodbye using the word *toodles*.

Lily took the report from the young coroner. The young man's hands were noticeably shaking. No doubt this was the first time he'd had to do an autopsy on a Caucasian. It was often a trying experience for Han Chinese. The very size of white people, even lying inert on a metal table, could be daunting. Then there was the smell. Han Chinese eat very few, if any, dairy products. The Caucasian diet of milk, cheese, yogurt, etc., leaves, to the Han Chinese olfactory sense, a most unpleasant odour on the skin. Then, of course, there was the fact of the suicide, so un-Chinese. At least for males.

Lily thanked the young man and indicated that he was to leave the room. She looked at Geoff's body. The handsome face, the inevitable thickening of middle age, the long – almost elegant – fingers. She briefly examined the ligature marks on the neck and compared them to the data she had about the rope that was in her office with the rest of the physical evidence. Then she checked for defensive wounds. Nothing. No skin under his nails, no cuts to either his skin or the clothing that he had worn.

She examined the clothes. Well worn but not terribly expensive jeans, a vest – odd to wear in the heat – a broadcloth shirt with a Bloomingdale's label. Lily knew from her CNN-watching that this was an expensive American store. The shirt, like the jeans, was well worn. Underwear, standard North American issue. It was his shoes that struck her as odd. They were of some sort of soft but durable light-brown leather with a thong shoelace. Totally flat on the bottom with shoemaker's nails in the soles. They had been handmade; machines didn't leave the heads of nails visible. She lifted the shoes and was surprised by their light weight. Then she held them away from her face and was again surprised, this time by the pleasing fact of their dimensions. There were the normal kind of scuff marks that shoes pick up and a bit of paint on the outside edge of the right shoe.

She put the shoes down and looked at the body again. For the first time, it occurred to her that she had a relationship, no matter how tenuous, to this entity on her autopsy table. Fong had been her first husband. Fong's first wife, Fu Tsong, had loved this man. Lily had loved Fong. Fong had loved Fu Tsong. Fu Tsong had loved Geoffrey Hyland. It creeped her out.

She took out her cell phone and called Chen. His voice was reassuring. It was wonderful to live with someone who was thrilled just to hear from you. They chatted briefly about the investigation then Chen asked about her daughter, Xiao Ming. She told him that her mother was baby-sitting and had promised not to play mah-jong. The slamming down of the tiles bothered the child.

Chen laughed. She loved that. He found her funny, he found her beautiful, he found her infinitely desirable. She found him just right for her present needs. She ended the conversation and returned to the report.

The alcohol level in Geoff's body was high but not extraordinary, unless he wasn't much of a drinker. She made a note to check. She flipped the pages of a basically negative toxicology report then stopped as something leapt out at her.

There had been a stain on his underclothing. It was seminal fluid mixed with Nonoxynol. Lily grabbed her book on chemi-

cal compounds and began to search. There was very little information on Nonoxynol except that it was an anti-organic – a
toxic substance used to eliminate growth. No specific uses were
named. She grabbed her pharmacology book and repeated her
search. Nonoxynol wasn't even listed.

She closed the book and thought. Whatever this was, it was
mixed with seminal fluid, so probably had something to do
with sex. Lily didn't know much about Western contraceptive
practices but she knew where to look. Six minutes of Google
later and she had her answer. Nonoxynol was the active ingre-
dient in a commercially sold spermicide. But few Chinese
women used spermicide as part of their usual contraceptive
practices. Lily wondered if maybe, with the new affluence of
Shanghai, younger Chinese women were now using this kind
of expensive product. She didn't know.

Yet here it was and mixed with Geoff's seminal fluids. She
looked back at the body. Could this man have been having sex
literally moments before he committed suicide? She picked up
the phone and called Fong.

His voice mail picked up. "Call me, Short Stuff. Surprise big
got I for you," she said in her own version of English.

Fong stood very still in the centre of Geoff's room. Despite the
man's many visits to Shanghai and his considerable success,
Geoff was still classified as a worker. Foreign worker, true, but
worker nonetheless. So the room he was assigned on the academy's grounds was adequate although hardly posh.

Fong drew open the curtain. The back of the ancient prop
shop was across the way. Its shutters were thrown wide in a
vain effort to combat the heat of the day. The sounds of ham-
mering something into submission filled the air. As Fong
watched, an elderly technician came out, lit up a smoke and
began to sew a leather pouch together.

Fong turned back to the room. Bed, night table, small desk,

laptop computer running a screen saver of fish swimming away from a big lazy shark, clothes hung on a rod. Books in the corners, on the floor beside the bed, on the night table. Video cassettes on the desk and two notepads. A small television with adaptor and slot for a VHS tape on the floor by the window.

Fong lifted the mattress and quickly established that there was nothing of interest there. He pulled it aside and went through the bedding and the pillows and the box spring. Nothing ripped, nothing opened, nothing there. Tossing them all in a corner, he knelt and ran his hands over the floorboards. They had probably been put down more than two hundred, maybe three hundred, years ago. It would be a clever man indeed who could prise one up and not leave telltale marks. There were none.

He reassembled the bed and quickly headed into the bathroom. More cosmetics than Fong would have thought. Some he couldn't identify but nothing hidden there.

He returned to the bedroom. He went through the clothing roughly. Nothing.

He tilted the lamp and unscrewed the bulb. Nothing.

He stacked things on the bed so he could reach the overhead fixture. Nothing.

He pulled off the faceplates of the electrical outlets. Nothing.

He pulled off the back of the television and fished around inside, careful not to touch the capacitor. Nothing.

He went into the bathroom and threw water on his face. When he looked up, he saw himself in the mirror – older than he thought of himself. Older than he knew he was. Behind him in the mirror were Geoff's cosmetics, kept in a rack in the shower.

Fong returned to the bedroom. The tapes, the books and the computer.

He sat on the bed and grabbed the hardcover books that were on the night table beside Geoff's Arden edition of *Hamlet*.

Geoff was evidently reading three novels by a man named le Carré. John le Carré. A Frenchman named John? Fong flipped over the jacket of the first book and read about Mr. le Carré's background. An English spy turned writer. Fong couldn't quite see a Chinese man doing that. Maybe that's why the guy changed his name when he wrote.

Fong put the three novels on the bed in front of him. *Tinker Tailor Soldier Spy*, *Our Game* and *The Secret Pilgrim*. He opened the first one and looked at the title page. Geoff had said something to him about tinkers and tailors. Fong remembered. That's what Geoff had said about the two guards in the first scene of his *Hamlet*. But he had said nothing about soldiers and spies. He held the book upside down and riffled through the pages. Nothing fell out. He then leafed through it. A few things were underlined, but it quickly became clear that Geoff was noting syntax and language usage, not actual subject matter as none of the underlined sections seemed to relate to any other.

In *The Secret Pilgrim*, Geoff had underlined a lot of the dialogue between a character called Ned and a man who endured capture by the Khmer Rouge in order to rescue his daughter. But it was in the third book, *Our Game*, that Geoff's slashing notes were everywhere. It was getting late. Fong turned on the light, sat back on the bed and began to read. Twenty pages in he saw Geoff's note: *I'm Tim!!!*

Our Game tells the story of a middle-aged British spy – Tim – who loses his younger wife to another spy who betrays his country and ends up fighting alongside the Chechens in the former Soviet Union. The final image is of Tim picking up a rifle and joining the rebel band – at long last "doing" something with his life. Fong finished skimming the book as the sun rose. Geoff's notes were all over the text – some underlinings, some in the margins, many right across the print itself. All were urgent, emphatic. Fong found it sentimental. Dangerously romantic. So unlike the Geoff he thought he knew.

"I am Tim. . . . So, what romantic calling were you on, Geoff?" Fong said aloud. Not surprisingly, no one answered.

Fong got off the bed, stretched, then phoned the office and left a message for Captain Chen to get in touch with him. He snapped his cell phone shut and looked back at the room. His eyes lit on the important remaining items: Geoff's copy of *Hamlet*, the VHS tapes and the laptop. He sat at the small desk and opened Geoff's copy of *Hamlet*. He was surprised how few notes were there. Fu Tsong's Shakespearean scripts had been a flurry of personal impressions and questions. Geoff's notes, written in a tight and concise hand so unlike the slashed comments in *Our Game*, appeared only four times in the entire text.

The first note was at the end of act one where Hamlet has received the information from the ghost about his father's death. There, Geoff wrote: *Could it be that Hamlet now has direction in his life – is happy?* The second was in the Polonius scene with Reynaldo where Geoff penned the simple word: *Spy*. The third was in act four when the story of Hamlet's escape from the plotting of Rosencrantz and Guildenstern is told. There, Fong was astounded to see Geoff's note: *Switch! Should I tell Fong?* And Geoff's last note was in the final act upon Hamlet's death: *Suicide? Suicide as failure? Suicide as success?*

A knock on Geoff's door brought Fong to his senses. Chen entered, surprised to see that Fong had clearly spent the night there.

"What's the time?"

"Just before eight, sir."

"Contact Li Chou. Get his people in here. Arrange a full meeting – Lily, Li Chou and his people, our guys – one o'clock."

Fong stood up.

"Did you find a suicide note, sir?"

Fong looked at Captain Chen, "I don't know. Maybe in its own way, I did." He headed toward the door.

"Where are you going, sir?"

"Home. I need a few hours of sleep before the meeting. Hand me those videotapes and notepads. You work on Mr. Hyland's laptop, Chen. I want to know everything that's on there."

Chen pulled out a small rectangular electronic gadget of some sort, detached a metal stick and touched the screen with it.

"What's that, Chen?

"It's called a PalmPilot, sir. It's really quite useful."

Fong nodded although he had no idea what something called a PalmPilot could be useful for.

"It keeps notes, sir, calendars and the like. And it can even be programmed to monitor radio signals."

Fong smiled and nodded but thought, "Fine, Chen, you use that thing. For me, I'll use a datebook to keep appointments and a radio to get radio signals."

At his apartment, Fong was grateful that the water had come back on. While the small gas water heater attached to the shower did its work, he returned to the bedroom and slid one of the tapes into his VHS adaptor then into his machine. He punched the On button. A program called *Six Feet Under* came up. Fong watched, trying hard not to yawn. When he got the gist of the show, he let the tape run and headed toward the shower.

The water was scalding hot but Fong didn't care. He put his face up to the pounding heat and allowed it to punish him in the hope it would take away his weariness. Over the sound of the water and the gas heater, he heard the VHS tape droning on. Between gurgles, he caught snippets of dialogue. Something about a cat. Something about these tits cost a fortune. Something about do you know who this was?

Fong reached for the soap and turned off the water to conserve gas. He began to lather up. Then stopped. No sound was coming from the VHS tape. Maybe this was an M.O.S. section. He smiled when he remembered Fu Tsong's explanation of the term: "*Mit* out sound, Fong."

"*Mit* out sound, what language is that?"

"Well, it's English with a German accent. Lots of the early Hollywood directors were German and *mit* is the German word for *with*. So without sound became *mit* out sound. M.O.S. – and it stuck."

Then a loud cackle of a microphone being tapped came from the VHS tape.

Geoff's voice said, "Don't do that." Then, "Three, two, one – play."

A beat of silence.

Then he heard her. His deceased wife, Fu Tsong – as clear as he heard her inside his head every time he entered a theatre: *"Here's flowers for you; Hot lavender, mints, savoury, marjoram; The marigold, that goes to bed wi' the sun and with him rises weeping' these flowers of middle summer, and I think they are given to men of middle age."*

Then she giggled, "I'm too old to play Perdita.

Fong felt himself stagger. His hand reached out and hit the water tap.

Then Geoff's voice responded, "Nonsense. Westerners can't tell the age of Asian women. Until they get old, that is."

"Are you suggesting that I'm old?"

"No. Never will you get old. Not to me."

The boiling hot water pelted down on Fong but he didn't move. Couldn't move, as Fu Tsong returned to her speech: *"I would I had some flowers o' the spring that become your time of day."* And then he was crying. The water mixing with his tears and swirling down the drain into the nothingness beneath.

Li Chou looked at the crime-scene photos of Geoff Hyland, then pushed them to one side and took a large, sealed manila envelope from his briefcase. The envelope had belonged to his CSU predecessor and Fong's close friend, Wang Jun. As part of Li Chou's deal in accepting the post, he had demanded all private papers that could be found from Wang Jun's time as head of the CSU. This was the only extant copy of Wang Jun's confidential report on the death of Fu Tsong. It had been found after Wang Jun's death, hidden in the man's mattress.

Li Chou slid the long nail of his left pinky finger along the crease of the envelope, opening the thing as easily as any letter opener could. The opening sentence of Wang Jun's report brought a smile to Li Chou's lips: *Fu Tsong, Zhong Fong's wife, was having an affair with the Canadian theatre director Geoffrey Hyland.*

In Li Chou's mind, he ticked off one of the three ingredients necessary for a murder to take place: motive.

"For the flowers now, that frighted thou let'st fall from Dis's waggon! Daffodils, that come before the swallow dares, and take the winds of March with beauty."

Fong stood before the image on the screen. Entranced. Unable to reach over and turn it off. Wanting it to last forever.

"Violets dim, but sweeter than the lids of Juno's eyes or Cytherea's breath; pale primroses that die unmarried, ere they can behold bright Phoebus in his strength – a malady most incident to maids; bold oxlips and the crown imperial: lilies of all kinds, the flower-de-luce being one! O, these I lack, to make you garlands of, and my sweet friend, to strew him o'er and o'er."

Fu Tsong's image held, suspended in digital space, her arms raised, her face alive with joy and then it was gone.

The phone rang so loudly that Fong jumped.

"Short stuff?"

"Lily?"

"Did you get my message?"

"Not yet."

"Pick up your messages. I don't leave them for my health, Short Stuff."

"I will, Lily."

"Good. When?"

"As soon as you answer a single question for me?"

"Sure. Xiao Ming is fine. You can pick her up early on Sunday if you want."

"Thanks. I look forward to that."

"So does she."

Fong was pleased. Although it wasn't easy, he and Lily were working their way to an understanding on how to share the raising of their daughter.

"But that's not my question, Lily."

"Well spit it out, Short Stuff." He did wish she'd stop calling him that although it was true she usually only used that appellation for him in private. What's your question, Fong?"

"What kind of flowers were on Geoff Hyland's body?"

Fong fast-forwarded through the VHS tapes. There were no more speeches by Fu Tsong. Just lots and lots of *Six Feet Under*. Fong mulled that over – lots and lots of *Six Feet Under*. Why was Geoff all of a sudden interested in a program about dying. I AM TIM and dying. *Soldier Sailor Tinker . . . Spy*.

Fong began to leaf through Geoff's notepads. In the back of the first one he found six typed pages filled with edits. As he read, he realized that this was Geoff's writing: *In the end all there is, is love. Every scene is about it, every character seeks it, every being lives in the hope of it."* Said by some old acting teacher, don't ask me who.

I have been teaching professional actors for over 20 years. I began to teach in New York between directing jobs in the American regional theatres. I taught in my Manhattan apartment three nights a week – my wife was very patient. In my second year of teaching, I was contacted by a young man from Yonkers. He asked if I would teach him and three of his friends. I asked about his background. He was not an amateur but he was clearly not travelling on a traditional professional trajectory. What he clearly was – was hungry. So I agreed.

On that first night, he showed up with his three friends, one of whom was a dark-eyed girl whose anger was so close to the surface that her face was in almost constant motion – as if whatever boundaries she had to keep the anger in check had been breached.

That first class we talked through some basic concepts, did a bit of improvisation and broke down a simple text. Then I suggested that we find scenes to work on. The girl told me that she wanted to watch a little first. I said that was okay but she would have to get up and perform in the class after next. She agreed. I gave the three young men a copy of David Mamet's **American Buffalo** and told them to prepare some of it for next week.

When we parted, they handed over the money for class. As a teacher, it was something that I will never forget. It was obvious the money they gave me, was "food money." As they left my apartment, I looked at the money and thought of the responsibility it imposed on me – and to be frank – it frightened me.

It was the beginning of my understanding that it was no longer good enough, as a teacher, to deliver hashed-over versions of the old acting dogma. That their "food money" obliged me to reassess what it was I was teaching. That too frightened me because there had been precious little, if any, serious reassessing within the acting teaching community for many, many years.

The following week, my Yonkers kids showed up on time and announced that they were ready to show me **American Buffalo**. I said, sure, assuming that they had put a few pages of the play on its feet. They started into the play — from the top. They did the whole play cover to cover, without a break. What they did manage to break in the course of their performance was the mirror over the mantelpiece, a lamp and a windowpane. When they were finished, they turned to me as if to say: So what do you think, Coach?

What I thought was that hunger was an important part of being *a professional actor and that these young hungry actors deserved better understanding of their art than there was available in the present acting texts.*

That was the beginning of the thinking that led to this book.

Three of these four aggressive young actors barged their way into the profession. The fourth – well . . . anger out of its cage – decompartmentalized, if you will – can be terribly destructive.

That was one of the few times in my life that I have taught beginner actors. I still don't teach beginners and this book is not intended for beginner actors, although if you have enough hunger, you'll be able to use the ideas and methods outlined in this book to make you a better actor.

Like most good ideas, the concepts in this book are easy to learn but may take quite a while to apply. It is easy enough to learn the rules of chess. It takes a lifetime to gain any mastery of the game.

Nothing of any value can be put on a 3-by-5 index card – except the thought that nothing of any value can be put on a 3-by-5 index card.

Acting teaching can be roughly broken down into those explorations that are about finding notes on an actor's piano keyboard and those explorations that are about how to play the notes that an actor has already discovered. This book, and my work for the past 20 years, is primarily about how to play the notes you have found. How to understand what the notes you have mean, which notes are not good any longer, which have never been good, which notes can replace bad notes, which notes are available to you but you don't know it – and most important – how to finger your stops and depress your frets so that you can play the notes you have together in a fashion that as Hamlet says "will discourse most eloquent music." (Hamlet, Act 3, Sc. 2)

The actor's territory is the human heart. It is an uncharted land defended by terrifying dragons but it also contains great glories, music and deep human truths. To the hungry actor it is the only land worthy of investigating.

This book attempts to give the actor a compass and survival kit for that strange land. It includes sketch maps and points of reference in that divine territory – whose exploration can for the artist, and should, last a lifetime.

Fong put down the pages. Who writes an introductory chapter to a book based on the knowledge gained in a lifetime of work and then commits suicide?

The next page was blank. The page after that was not. This page was filled with Geoff's red felt-pen scratchings. The top part of the page seemed to be an effort to write a section on "being present," a term that Fu Tsong had often used. But that ended quickly and was replaced with a set of large angry words: *How, with her gone? How? How the fuck without her!*

Fong felt sick. He had no doubt who the "her" was that Geoff referred to. It was his dead wife and Geoff's dead lover – Fu Tsong.

CHAPTER SIX

 RESPONSE

eoff's death was duly noted by some of the Canadian press, but because he had done much of his work in the United States the notices were small, buried and perfunctory. Had he been either a member of one of the Old Anglo families who still ran the theatre world in Canada or had he spent six weeks in Czechoslovakia, rather than sixteen years in America, his death would have been worthy of several column inches in the entertainment sections and would no doubt have been followed by engaging eulogies delivered by middle-aged ponytailed men.

One theatre that had contracted Geoff to direct in the upcoming season actually breathed a sigh of relief at his passing. The artistic director had promised his business manager a show to direct but had overlooked this obligation after the acting company raised a considerable fuss. But Geoff's death provided the answer gift-wrapped – Geoff was gone, we had tried to get him to direct but he was gone and at this late date who could we possibly get – hey, the business manager is available – aren't we all one big happy family again!

There was one other place in Canada that Geoff's passing was noted – although not publicly. It was on the West Coast of the huge country on a mountaintop university campus by a handsome man in his late thirties who went by the name Richard Lee. He dressed and moved casually, but there was a real distance in his eyes. As if something far-off were the object of his attention.

That something far-off was in fact his brother, Xi Luan Tu.

Richard sat on the wooden deck on the north side of the Simon Fraser University campus and stared at the snow-covered peaks across the way. The dazzling sunlight, a rarity for this part of the world even in summer, flooded over him. He had come to Simon Fraser University because of the significant Dalong Fada presence on the campus, which allowed him to arrange for adequate security for his meeting. And therefore he sat, at the appointed hour, in the brilliant sunshine, on this campus – almost empty of people – and read the university's promotional brochure. Richard was not interested in the university's self-congratulatory bibble-babble about its achievements and its goals, but he found the short blurb on the history of the school's namesake, Simon Fraser, really quite interesting. It seemed that all Mr. Fraser managed to accomplish in his life was to be the first Caucasian to enter the land that is now called British Columbia. He accomplished this overland feat in 1808 at the behest of the North West Company of Montreal. It appears, though, that the company was looking for beaver pelts, not some of the world's most spectacular country. He had failed in his appointed task. He was a man who discovered beauty but not rodents.

A large raven, inky blue-black, fluttered to a stop on a nearby concrete ledge and looked at Richard. The bird's sharp beak snapped open and emitted a flat caw. Richard held the bird's eyes. Two black pebbles in a deeper darkness. In Mandarin, Richard said, "Fly away without my soul today and I will pray to you tomorrow."

"Not a classic Dalong Fada thought," said a sharp voice in Mandarin from behind Richard. The raven cawed loudly again and flapped its wings but maintained its roost on the post.

Richard turned toward the source of the voice. The man standing there was in his mid-to-late twenties; the results of a fairly regular attendance in a weight room were evident on his arms, chest and neck. He held a fresh croissant in one hand. He wore expensive Italian slacks and a pure linen shirt. But his feet, exposed by his ever-so-fashionable sandals, were pure Hunan peasant.

"How does a boy from the rice paddies get all the way to a university atop a mountain in Canada?" asked Richard.

"The cause. And you?"

Richard canted his head slightly to indicate that "the cause" had brought him here too, but they both knew they came for very different aspects of the cause. The two men stared at each other. The raven moved its cold eyes from one to the other.

Finally, the younger man took a bite from the croissant and said, "I got your note."

"Good."

"Are we betrayed?"

Richard looked away. "I don't know. Xi Luan Tu is still in Shanghai. I don't know if this Canadian theatre director betrayed him before they hanged him or not."

"You're sure he was hanged then?"

"No, I'm not sure," he spat back then softened his tone as he continued, "but he had a cell phone with wireless Internet access programmed to get Xi Luan Tu most of the information he would need to get out of China. Mr. Hyland smuggled it into Shanghai on his first trip but never got it to Xi Luan Tu. He went back to deliver the phone as well as the money and papers he smuggled in this second time. Then he contacts us to tell us that the phone is safe but he had to jettison the money and the papers, and shortly thereafter he is swinging from a rope." He picked up a pebble and thought of throwing it at the raven then decided to toss it over the edge of the platform.

"The connective seems clear to me. Besides I don't believe in coincidence, do you?"

"No."

"Good. We have to move quickly now. Xi Luan Tu and many others are probably in great danger. Who knows what Mr. Hyland told the authorities before they hanged him. We must send someone else in there with the money and the papers Xi Luan Tu needs to get him out of there."

"Do we have an operative who can manage that?"

"Yes." Richard looked out at the mountains. "She won't like it, but it's time to activate her for the sake of her dead lover."

"The fireman?"

"Yes."

"Where's she, now?"

"In Hong Kong."

"Still with the police force?" the young man asked unable to hide the suspicion in his voice.

"She's an arson investigator there, not exactly a normal cop."

"You want me to contact her?"

"No. I'll do it, but I want you to activate your people in Shanghai. We may need their help to rescue Xi Luan Tu."

The younger man nodded then tossed a piece of the croissant to the raven. The bird ignored it and stared at the Chinese men as if wondering what could have brought these two to his domain.

"Fly to my brother," Richard said in his heart. "Tell him we're coming to get him." To the surprise of both men the great bird cawed loudly, flapped its wings and took flight. Richard watched him ascend a thermal then head east. "From the Golden Mountain to the Middle Kingdom," Richard thought, but said nothing.

Richard took a deep breath and allowed himself a moment of

reflection. A looking back at the tumult of events that had brought him inevitably to this mountaintop university on the outskirts of Vancouver Canada. He knew that Dalong Fada is now the popular name for the movement that is one tradition within Xulian, ancient methods to cultivate the mind and keep the body healthy. Years ago, however, Xulian picked up a religious association, so groups adopted a new word for their practices – *qigong* (*qi* meaning life energy and *gong* meaning cultivation of energy). But Richard realized that Dalong Fada, no matter what its name, is far more than the series of physical exercises that structure the centre of the practice. As its leader has admitted, Dalong Fada is a way of life. Its methods of insight and health for the body and mind have attracted a large and loyal following.

Every successful political movement (and since its modern inception in the early nineties, Dalong Fada has been incredibly successful, growing from a few practitioners to many millions of followers) gets to a point where it is seen as an opponent to the power structure. When that happens, those in power attack the upstart movement. The movement then splinters into those who propel its values and ideas and those who protect those values and ideas. It's the inevitable division in any successful movement between faith and force. For the faithful, like Richard, it becomes the classic deal with the devil, in this case, the military arm of Dalong Fada, which is under the control of the young peasant from Hunan Province – the young man with the fancy clothes and open-toed sandals.

The sound of young women's voices made Richard turn. Over by the reflecting pool with the obscenely large piece of jade in its centre, three young women had taken off their tops and hopped into the water to cool themselves. "What would they do to cool themselves off in the stifling heat and humidity that is a Shanghai summer," Richard wondered, "remove their skins?"

The e-mail wasn't a surprise to Joan Shui, but it threw her world into a tailspin, like a plane whose jet engine had just ingested a large bird.

It was too soon. Wu Fan-zi, her Shanghanese lover, had only been dead seven months. His birthday, which she had celebrated with Fong and the Canadian lawyer Robert Cowens, was the last time she'd been in Shanghai.

She curled in on herself. She thought for a moment about pulling out her phonebook – what she used to think of as her book of dates. Comfort, the oblivion of sex, being the object of desire seemed momentarily the only way out.

Shanghai. Fuck. She looked at her recently refurnished condo on the forty-third floor of her building on Hong Kong's Braemar Hill Road. This was real. Shanghai was . . . she didn't know the right word for what Shanghai was, but she really wasn't sure that she was ready to go back there yet. Wu Fan-zi's face would be everywhere she looked.

And this time, Fong would be the enemy.

She checked her coded e-mail message a second then a third time. They definitely wanted her in Shanghai and no doubt they knew how to get her there. There was a long list of instructions, but the gist of them was that she was to deliver money and papers that would aid in the escape of Dalong Fada's foremost organizer – Xi Luan Tu, Richard Lee's brother. And, by the by, China's most wanted man.

CHAPTER SEVEN

MEMORIES AND MEETINGS

After unceremoniously kicking Shrug and Knock out of the sweltering meeting room, Fong sat at one end of the large oval table waiting for the others to arrive. At least there hadn't been any evidence on the table for Shrug and Knock to snoop at. "Count the small blessings," he reminded himself as he allowed his mind to drift. First to other meetings in this room then to a place in his memory he hadn't visited for a very long time. He was sitting across his office desk from a middle-aged Englishman. Alternating waves of guilt and relief crossed the man's handsome angular face. "You can go now, Mr. Paulin," Fong repeated. "We know you didn't have anything to do with the death of your wife. You were lucky." The man stood slowly and headed toward the door. Fong rose from his chair. When he did, Mr. Paulin stopped in mid-stride as if suddenly he had become the icon for "Walk."

Fong said, "We know you didn't kill your wife, Mr. Paulin, but we know you wanted her dead. To be exact, we know that you were getting ready to plan her death, but an out-of-control taxi on Wolumquoi Lu solved your problem, didn't it?"

Mr. Paulin didn't move – couldn't move – as if a brittle wire from Fong's heart to his connected the two men. Then the wire snapped. Mr. Paulin reassumed his stature and looked down on Fong – not just from a height but from a long-held sense of racial superiority. "Can I go, Officer, or is there something else you want to say to me?"

"You can go, Mr. Paulin."

"Good."

"But don't think of coming back to Shanghai, Mr. Paulin."

The man whirled on Fong, clearly about to defend his right as a British citizen to come and go as he wished, to do business where he damned well pleased – but all he said was, "Anything else?"

"Yes." Fong made him wait for it. Then on the off breath he said, "Murder eats away the heart. It was only chance that saved you from killing your wife. Don't forget that. And remember that chance does us a favour once but charges us twice. You owe fortune twice now, Mr. Paulin."

Fong held out the man's passport. "You'll need this to leave China. You have six hours to be gone from the Middle Kingdom. Starting from this very moment."

Mr. Paulin slammed the door as he left Fong's office. Fong counted to twenty then released his breath and turned to the window. On the other side of the glass was the world famous Bund and across the Huangpo River the Pudong, which was in short order becoming the very centre of the miracle of economic revival that was Shanghai. He looked at the shiny new buildings but was unimpressed. "Maybe just because I'm getting older," he said aloud to the empty room and leaned his head against the cool windowpane. He was having more and more trouble keeping the world's evil at bay. The mangled body of Mrs. Paulin that they had extracted from the wrecked taxicab would now wake in the morning with him and accompany him to sleep at night – as would the relieved look on her husband's face. So many souls tucked beneath his skin, fighting for space in the membranous sack around his heart. So much ghostly weight.

Fong looked up. The room was filled with officers waiting for him. He wondered how long he had indulged in his memory.

Li Chou was at the far end of the oval table. His men were on either side of him. Lily sat halfway up one side with her young assistant. Chen sat across from her with Fong's people.

Fong "*ahemed*" and the room quieted. Cigarette smoke hung in layered clouds in the room. The windows were open and the hazy saturated air of a Shanghai summer afternoon moved in and out like the water at the shore of a placid lake.

Fong looked around the table. He really didn't have any plan in mind. Just to get started.

"Lily?"

"Message pick up, did you?" she said in her own private version of English. She was about to add her pet phrase for him, "Short Stuff," then decided against it in public.

"No, I'm sorry but . . . "

"Fine. No nose off my teeth," she said.

He had no idea what that meant, but signalled that she should begin the proceedings. She opened a folder and handed out copies of the autopsy report and the toxicology data then said in her beautiful Mandarin, "If you look at the autopsy report, there is no evidence of previous trauma to the body. In other words, he wasn't killed then hanged. He was just hanged. There were elevated levels of alcohol in Mr. Hyland's bloodstream but they weren't high enough to make him lose contact with reality unless he really wasn't a drinker. Someone should check into that."

"I did," said Fong. "He wasn't a drunk or an abstainer, just a guy – he drinks, drank."

Lily nodded.

From a large plastic bag she took out the noose and tossed it on the table then said, "It has one less turn than a traditional hangman's noose but outside of that it's standard issue. The position of the ladder conforms to the mathematical paradigm of something that tall being pushed from that height. The rope was easily strong enough to strangle a man of Mr. Hyland's weight."

Fong looked up from his notes.

"Yes, sorry about that, but this man's neck wasn't snapped like in a proper hanging. He strangled to death. It probably took several minutes."

She paused as that sank in.

"That accounts for the ligature burns up and down Mr. Hyland's neck," she said.

Fong nodded and made a note. He wasn't sure Lily was right about that.

"There are threads of the hemp embedded in his fingers and palms, which seem to indicate that he fought the rope at the end."

Fong experienced a moment of real panic. He didn't want that image in his head. Geoff, dangling, trying to loosen the rope, trying to scream – no.

One of the detectives put down his copy of the report and said, "He changed his mind, you mean?"

"If . . . " Lily didn't complete her sentence.

Fong did. "If this was actually a suicide. Anything else, Lily?"

"There were no defensive wounds on the body. No skin under the nails. The only other toxicological findings of interest were traces of seminal fluid in his underclothing . . . " She paused for a moment as the usual smirks in response to ejaculation at the end of a life passed over the men's faces then she added, "mixed with Nonoxynol."

"What's that?" Fong asked.

"It's a spermicide." The men around the table looked blankly at Lily. None had any idea what she was talking about. Lily sighed her you-poor-benighted-pagans smile and said,

"Some Western women use it as a contraceptive. It seems Mr. Hyland had a little nooky-nooky sometime before his demise." Then to Fong in English she added, "On message, Short Stuff. Pickup no surprise. No pickup, surprise surprise."

"How long before his demise, Lily?" Fong asked.

"Not long. Soon details I get, then you get, you get me?"

Fong nodded. A ripple of confusion circled the table, but Fong didn't want to get sidetracked on that. "Anything else, Lily?"

"No," she said in Shanghanese.

"What about the flowers that were in his vest pocket?"

"Marigolds, forget-me-nots and primroses," Lily replied then added, "is there anything . . . "

Fong cut her off, "What about the vest itself?"

"What about it?"

"It was a thousand degrees that night. Why would he wear a vest?"

Lily shrugged then said, "Perhaps Mr. Hyland was a slave to fashion. Maybe he wanted to die looking his best."

"True, but who gets laid then kills himself?" asked Li Chou. "This was no suicide. I agree with Zhong Fong."

"Well, that's a first," Fong said in English to Lily, who raised an eyebrow in response.

"What was that, Zhong Fong?" Li Chou asked.

Fong smiled but wondered why Li Chou's pronunciation of his name sounded to his ears awfully close to Traitor Zhong. "You're up, Li Chou. What did you and your crew find?"

Li Chou opened a stained folder and spread out a series of documents. "There were literally fingerprints everywhere. Sixteen partials and twenty-seven full prints. We've finger-printed the theatre's technicians and actors and are slowly identifying whose prints are whose. However, with so many prints on the ladder it is unlikely that this line of investigation will yield anything of interest.

"The rope was actually cut from a stock of rope that was kept in the west side of the theatre. The cut on the tail of the rope there matches the head of the rope used to hang Mr. Hyland."

"I'm afraid there are small flesh deposits on the rope within reaching distance of the noose which supports Ms. Lily's supposition that the man suffocated."

Fong wondered why Li Chou was being so solicitous. What was with the "I'm afraid" part of his last statement? But before Fong could speak, Lily piped up, "I don't make suppositions, Mr. Li."

Li Chou's hands flew up like he was fending off mosquitoes on Good Food Street. "No criticism intended, Ms. Lily."

"That would be another first," Fong thought.

"Then there were these." He pushed a large plastic evidence bag marked *Floor Findings* onto the table. "Pretty normal stuff, nothing you wouldn't expect on a stage. A few makeup sticks, bits of torn cloth, cigarette butts, stick matches, a hair clip, three pages of some script, a sodden handkerchief, three small-denomination yuan notes, a paperclip, wood chips . . . "

Fong interrupted him, "Did Mr. Hyland have a rehearsal set up for that morning?"

"Yes," replied Captain Chen, referring to his notes. "No one was very happy about it. Apparently once a theatrical production starts to perform it is considered bad form to . . . "

"Who was called?"

"Called?"

"Told to be at rehearsal," Fong clarified.

Li Chou gave him a who-cares look.

Fong ignored him and looked to Chen, "I want to see everyone who Geoff called to rehearsal for that morning."

Chen made a note and flipped open his cell, "Odd to call a rehearsal then kill yourself, don't you think?"

Fong could have added, "Odd to start writing a book then kill yourself," but he didn't.

"Odd indeed, unless you wanted those called to rehearsal to come in and find you still swinging." It was the commissioner who snuck noiselessly into the room behind Fong. The man had changed his demeanour of late. The rumour in the station was that he was modelling himself after the new actor who played the head of the district attorney's office on the American television show *Law and Order* – not the original one, but the one who followed the lady who played it for a bit. Fong had never seen the program, but apparently it was very popular throughout Shanghai. For an instant he wondered if Fu Tsong would have liked the show. The man continued, "An odd sort of 'up yours' but, I imagine, in some people's eyes, a very effective one."

The commissioner shifted his position in the doorway to catch the light better or something. It unnerved Fong that he hadn't at least sensed the man's presence.

"Still to kill yourself like that?" the commissioner pressed on.

"True, sir," Fong said, "but there is every possibility that this was not a suicide."

"If it's not then someone went to serious dramatic lengths to make us believe it was a suicide."

"Very dramatic lengths," said Fong.

"Who? Who would do this?"

"That would be the question, wouldn't it, sir?" said Fong.

The man's clothes may have changed and maybe even his demeanour but his uncanny ability to state the obvious as if he had revealed some great truth had remained firmly intact.

"Carry on," the commissioner said and turned on his heel.

Fong was sure that if he could have seen the man's face he would have watched a self-satisfied smile cross his lips. He'd managed to set the investigation on firm legs. Oh yes he had. And now he could tell whomever it is he reports to that he had done the best he could with what meagre resources, both financial and human, he'd been given. It was a classic bit of ass covering.

Then Fong noticed Li Chou's face – he was calm, serene. It scared the shit out of Fong.

Fong took a breath and turned to Lily, "How many steps up the ladder would he have to have climbed to get his head into that noose?"

"Eleven, maybe twelve, Fong."

"And how heavy was Mr. Hyland?"

"Fong?"

"How much did he weigh, Lily?"

"Just under a hundred and eighty pounds."

Fong thought about that for a bit. How do you get a 180-pound man to climb twelve steps up a ladder? Then once he's up there, how do you get him to put his head in a noose? Then how do you get down the ladder before he takes the noose off his neck and follows you down?

Fong shot to his feet. The words *I ascend* literally propelled him up. Everyone in the room looked at him but he didn't care. His mind was on himself and Chen by the pinrail. And the counterweights. Christ and counterweights: "I ascend."

He smiled as the memory he couldn't pull forward at the time bloomed full force in his head. She was laughing. Fu Tsong, his wife, was laughing. No, she was roaring with laughter. Laughter was literally thundering out of her mouth so that Fong couldn't understand what she was saying. They were sitting on the Bund Promenade. She had just come back from adjudicating a drama festival in Taipei. Fong wanted to hear her impressions of the renegade island. She wasn't interested in talking about that. She wanted to tell him about what she had seen in the theatre – except her laughter kept getting in the way.

"Just take a breath and tell me," Fong had said.

She did – take a breath, that is. Her laughter stopped then it erupted once again.

Fong got up. Immediately, someone took his seat. This was Shanghai – public seating of any sort was at a premium. He looked at the old lady who had taken his place but before he could speak she said, "Tough luck, Flat Head."

How did they always know he was a cop?

Suddenly Fu Tsong leaned over and whispered something into the old lady's ear. The crone's face went dark then she got up and moved along. Fong couldn't recall ever being able to move someone from a seat on the Bund Promenade before. As he reassumed his seat, he asked, "What did you say to her, Fu Tsong?"

"I told her I had the plague."

"You didn't."

"You're right, I didn't. I told her that you were my sweet hard-working husband and you needed to rest your weary feet."

"That wouldn't have moved her even an inch."

"True."

"So?"

"So I told her that if she didn't move her fat ass I'd put my fingers up her nose and pull it off her face."

"You said that?"

"I did."

"And she believed you?"

Fu Tsong unwrapped a sticky confection and put it in her mouth. "You might recall that I'm a very good actress, Fong," she said as she munched the gooey thing.

"You are," said Fong as he looked anew at his wife. Would there ever be a time when she didn't surprise him?

"So what happened in those plays you had to adjudicate in Taipei?"

"Play, you mean," she said as she swallowed the candy.

"Do I?"

"You do. I saw the same play thirteen times done by thirteen different groups."

"Was that what was so funny?"

"Hardly. Watching the same play over and over again is tedious."

"Unless it's a great play."

"Or done by great actors under an inspired director. But no Fong, this adaptation of the *Wakefield Crucifixion* is not a great play, and these were not great actors and there wasn't a director to be seen in the group."

"What's a *Wakefield Crucifixion*?"

"It's a religious play from England."

"Modern?"

"No. What they call the Dark Ages."

"Ah, the time that the Russians think didn't really exist."

"Right, Fong. You really are a font of truly useless information."

"I'll take that as a compliment."

"I wouldn't. Anyway, in this play, which was being done by church groups – they didn't tell me that when they asked me to adjudicate their drama festival nor did they tell me that they were amateurs, Christian amateurs. Anyway, in this play, Christ gathers his followers, he pisses off the authorities, they whip him, crucify him, bury him and then he . . . " she burst out laughing.

"He what?" Fong demanded.

By now several dozen people had gathered round to hear the story.

"Okay," Fu Tsong pulled herself together and said, "he ascends." She broke into peels of laughter.

"To where, does he ascend?" Fong demanded to get her to stop laughing.

"To the Christian heaven or something. How would I know?"

"Okay, so he ascends. What's so funny?"

"Well, the ascending happens at the end of the second act.

Each group attaches a harness of some sort to the actor playing Christ and the play ends by him saying 'I ascend' and he is gently pulled up to the fly gallery above the proscenium arch. It's hokey but cute."

"I still don't get what's so funny."

"Well, to do the 'ascending' smoothly, you have to have counterweights on the flylines that pretty much match the weight of the actor."

"Yes," Fong said, prompting.

"Well, on the third day – I was seeing four productions a day and five on the last day – well, on the third day, in the third performance I'd seen that day, a very large actor was playing Christ and it was obvious to me that he was not feeling well. He literally sneezed and coughed his way through the entire first act. I think he fainted at intermission. So at the beginning of the second act the stage manager came out and announced that the poor boy was too ill to go on and that his understudy would fill in for the second act." Fu Tsong began to laugh. Fong gave her a stern look. She stopped laughing. "Well, the understudy Christ was not a big boy like the first-act Christ. In fact, he was a pretty tiny boy."

Fong got it. "No!"

"Yes! They forgot to change the counterweights. So when this little guy put on the harness and announced all grave and serious 'I ascend,' shit Fong, he didn't ascend, he rocketed. He zoomed. He disappeared in a puff of smoke and we heard the smack of him hitting the fly gallery. A few moments later, his feet appeared below the proscenium arch and just hung there. Then the feet began to move and we heard this Christian god saviour shout, 'Get me the fuck down from here you moronic assholes!'"

Fong almost laughed but was glad he hadn't.

Everyone around the table was still looking at him. He turned to Li Chou, "Isolate those fingerprints. Did you print the counterweights by the pinrail?"

"No."

"How about the chair by the pinrail?"

"No, not that either, but I . . . "

"Do it. I want to know everyone who touched the ladder, the chair or the counterweights. I also want fibres collected from the ladder, the noose and the whole area around the counterweights on the pinrail."

To Fong's amazement, Li Chou leapt to his feet and signalling his men to follow him said, "Will do, Zhong Fong."

There it was again. Zhong Fong pronounced like Traitor Zhong.

Once Li Chou was gone, Fong turned to Chen, "Find out how the wooden batten that the rope was threaded through is lowered and who has control of that. While you're at it, test the pulleys. I want to know if they both work. I also want to know if there are prints on the pulleys."

"You still want to see the people called to rehearsal, sir?"

"And the actors last to leave the theatre that night."

"I've already arranged that."

"Good. What about that Shakespeare expert?"

"His contact numbers are on your desk."

"Good."

Chen divided up assignments among his men and headed out, leaving Fong alone with Lily. "You can tell Chen that he's allowed to look at you in these meetings. He's your husband."

"Chen is very formal. You are his superior officer, Fong. I may be his wife but this is a business meeting not a cocktail party."

"True, Lily," and without a beat of segue he asked, "What kind of paint was used in the theatre?"

"I don't know offhand. You want the paint used on the platforms or on the thing that . . . "

"The proscenium arch?"

"Yeah, you would know the name for that."

"I would. It's called the proscenium arch."

"Fine. So you want to know the kind of paint used on the arch?"

"Yes."

"Fine. I'll check."

"Good. Then would you check if it matches the smudge of paint on Mr. Hyland's right shoe?"

Lily looked at him with a wry expression on her face. "Sure, I can do that."

"How long to get that information, Lily?"

"Not long." Suddenly she shifted and leaned forward. "How are you managing, Fong?"

"Okay," he said, very uncomfortable to be talking like this.

"You miss Xiao Ming?"

"Yes. But I get to see her almost as much as I did when we . . . "

"Were married, Fong. You're allowed to say that."

"Yes." Fong began to pack up his things. "You look happy, Lily."

"I am Fong."

"I'm glad. I'll be on time picking up Xiao Ming Sunday."

"If this case is solved by then."

"Yes, Lily, if this case is solved by then."

Fong stopped packing up.

"Something I can help you with, Fong?"

"Yes. But I don't know what just yet."

"You'll let me know?"

"I will. . . . Lily . . . "

She stared at him closely, "What Fong?"

"What happens to people when they lose a sense of purpose?"

Fong went directly to his office. Captain Chen was waiting there. "Who's that, sir?" Chen asked, pointing at Shrug and

Knock who had stationed his desk across the hall from Fong's door. Fong ushered Chen into the office, closed the door and explained the who and what, if not the why, of Shrug and Knock. Chen nodded. "Men like him are a reality in the politics of this place. If you want to work here, you have to deal with the politics as well as the job but if you look at things closely, almost every situation can lead to either problems or opportunities. It's all a matter of seeing the possibilities."

Chen nodded. "Can I have a word, sir?"

"Sure, take a seat."

Chen sat then began without preamble, "So you believe this is not a suicide, sir?"

"Yes. I believe this was a murder made to look like a suicide."

"Are you sure, sir? How do you keep a noose on a man's neck, make him walk up ten steps of a ladder then kick the ladder aside. There were no signs of any real struggle. No defensive wounds, no . . . "

Fong cut him off. "Mr. Hyland never climbed that ladder. It was placed on the stage after Mr. Hyland was dead. Get me six men, access to the man who pulls those fly ropes and a hundred-and-eighty-pound dummy and I'll show you how it was done."

"Now?"

Fong looked at his watch. The theatre would just be opening. He had other things he could do before he proved his point, so he said, "No. Tomorrow. Get us in there tomorrow first thing."

CHAPTER EIGHT

THE VOYAGE OF JOAN SHUI

Joan Shui assumed she had been chosen because she was new to the movement and hence probably not known to the authorities. Authorities like her. Being a cop was probably another reason they had chosen her. She'd been a member of the Hong Kong constabulary for almost ten years. Before that, she'd done an advanced degree in chemistry. It was that degree that allowed her immediate entrance to the elite Hong Kong arson squad. Her father, the first fireman in her life, had been so proud. For a moment, she wondered if he would be proud of what she was about to do. "We can hardly please the living, how can we hope to please the dead?" she asked the emptiness of her office.

She looked out her office window. The deterioration of Hong Kong was subtle but it was there. It had started quickly after the mainland took back the British protectorate in 1996. At first it was just little things, neon signs that didn't flash, stores with shorter hours, vacancy rates rising, but of late the rot was threatening to break into the open. No longer was it just cosmetic. Something in the heart of Hong Kong could be dying.

That was why she was a supporter of Dalong Fada. She did believe in the exercise regime, but it was the fact of opposition to the Communists now that Hong Kong was no longer free that drew her to the movement. Without some form of opposition, Beijing would run even further amok then it had already. Dalong Fada was the only credible opposition in the entire country.

Her initial steps toward Dalong Fada had seemed so natural. A flirtation with a high-ranking member. A contact with an American-Chinese man. A series of discreet meetings and she was – a part of it.

Now there was a message and an assignment. For the briefest moment she wondered if this was what an al-Qaeda freak felt like. One moment a normal working stiff, the next a man with a bomb. Then she shook that off. She was not involved with bombs. Nothing that she was doing had anything to do with hurting people. She was a member of Dalong Fada because China needed a real opposition to the Chinese Communist Party – period, the end.

The phone on her desk rang. Joan let it ring as she remembered a call at almost exactly this time two days ago – when life was considerably simpler, a different reality. It had been a young lab technician with the results from her investigation of a fire on Peak Road. Insurance companies were taking a bath as fear of Beijing's control gripped Hong Kong and drove land values down. Many fashionable buildings were no longer financially viable. Better to burn them down and collect the insurance than to declare bankruptcy and face the shame, even in a financial centre like Hong Kong, that accompanied monetary failure.

Joan had nodded as she jotted down notes from the lab. Traces of accelerant had been found in the apartment building's basement. No planch was discovered, but the burn pattern was nothing if not suspicious. She thanked the technician and made a series of further requests for data. She sensed his hesitancy. "What?" she asked. The young man hemmed and hawed then finally said, "Are you doing anything Saturday night?" His question was no surprise to Joan. She was an attractive, unmarried, educated woman in her mid-thirties. She had a good job, beautiful if hard facial features and curves that attracted many eyes. What was she doing Saturday night? It was Wednesday. Did any who, who was any who in Hong Kong, have any idea what or who they were doing three days ahead? No. "Give me your cell number and I'll get back to you," she said to get him off the line. The young man evidently couldn't believe his good fortune. He had thanked her more than he should have and gave her not only his cell number, but also the apartment number of the place he shared with three men and even his mom's phone number.

The phone on her desk stopped ringing. Joan found the silence that followed strangely unnerving.

She pulled open a drawer of her desk and found the scrap of paper on which she'd scribbled the lab tech's numbers. He was clearly either too young or too stupid or both for her to date, but he might be just perfectly equipped to account for at least some of the days she'd be out of Hong Kong.

She put his phone numbers to one side and stood up. She looked around her. After what she was about to do, all of this could change – to be frank, it could be no more. She didn't know what she thought of that. She loved her work and she'd been adequately rewarded for her considerable expertise. Now she could be throwing it all away. She looked again at the coded e-mail from Dalong Fada and memorized the instructions and the single contact number there. She knew that once she dialled that number she might never be able to return to her life here. Before she met Wu Fan-zi in Shanghai she would never have considered giving all this up. But now, after Wu Fan-zi, she would. She picked up the phone and dialled the Dalong Fada number.

The phone was answered with a stiff "*Dui*." The use of Mandarin in Hong Kong was unusual, but it was what she expected. Quickly, in Mandarin, she gave the code words from the e-mail, "When does the Club Sierra open?"

"Just before moonrise," came the coded answer.

"Is the movie star dancing tonight?"

"*Dui.*"

The phone went dead. If someone tried to trace the call they would be out of luck. The person who answered Joan's call only used cell phones once then threw them into the sea.

Joan took a breath. The silly old British phrase *the game's afoot* popped into her head – a remnant from her British education that had featured second-, third-, and fourth-rate British writers above all others. She sat and dialled the young tech's number. She felt a little bad about using him – but only a little bad. "It's Joan Shui," she said. The pause that followed was probably the result of him dropping his cell phone. "Hey, how're you doin', hey?" he said in his best impression of a man in complete control.

It was not a terribly impressive impression.

"I've managed to clear the next few days. Are you busy?"

Splutter, pause, clunk, then, "Great. Good. No, great."

"How about three nights at the Calden Inn?"

The silence that followed was the longest yet. The poor lad was balancing his good fortune with the incredible expense of three nights at the Calden Inn. The Calden Inn was an exclusive private retreat just across from Macaw. Before Joan Shui had gone to Shanghai to investigate an arson in an abortion clinic and fallen hopelessly in love with Shanghai's head fireman Wu Fan-zi, she had thought that a weekend at the Calden Inn was the height of chic. Wealthy men sometimes suggested the Calden Inn as a great place for a little R and R and she sometimes took them up on it. Before Wu Fan-zi, she thought of sex much the same way as she thought of calisthenics – sometimes the exertion was very pleasing and sometimes it was less pleasing. The only consistent reality of her many visits to the Calden Inn was the pleasure she had given the men she was with and the luxury that they had provided for her.

"I've already made reservations in your name. I gave them your Visa number; we have it on file here for times that you have to go out of pocket for us. I got us a suite. I have to complete something here but I'll meet you out there first thing tomorrow morning. Okay?"

She didn't have to wait for an answer. She knew what it was going to be.

"Great. See you out there. Don't be late." She hung up then dialled the Calden Inn. She asked for the manager, who she'd befriended a few years back when she helped him solve a little arson-related unpleasantness in his kitchen.

"Ms. Shui, how nice to hear from you," the manager said with evident feeling.

"I have a favour to ask."

"Ask, please."

"My new boss . . ." – since the handover, Hong Kongers used the term to refer to totally incompetent but politically connected mainland overseers appointed by Beijing – ". . . has a son who just won't take no for an answer. He's booked a suite at your resort for three nights. When he arrives, I need you to claim that I came and found that he wasn't there on time so you assigned me my own private room in the other end of the building and that I have sworn you to secrecy so that under no circumstance will you tell him which room I am in."

"It is a large resort," he chuckled.

"And so very private."

"Indeed." He cleared his throat. "And were you particularly angry at the young man's tardiness?"

"Furious."

"As well you should be. I myself am almost beyond speaking

I am so profoundly upset by the actions of this young hellion."

"Thanks."

"My pleasure, Ms. Shui."

She hung up and made one more call. This to one of her snitches. Firebugs liked to brag – snitches were invaluable to arson inspectors.

"Now what?" came the snivelling voice over the cell phone. "You going to bust my balls over exactly what this time?"

Joan took a breath and asked sweetly, "Your balls grew back then?"

"Ha, ha! Lady cops! *Ye sheng!!!* Spare me from lady cops."

"You know where the main forensics lab is?"

"Near Qian Shui Wan?"

"Yeah."

"Okay, I know where it is," he said slowly.

"Good. Follow a young tech named Clarence Chi and very early Saturday morning, say between 1 and 2 a.m., put a sizeable quantity of sand into the gas tank of his car."

"And I get what out of this, exactly?"

"I conveniently lose the file on a certain restaurant robbery that took place last Tuesday."

"I thought you were arson."

"I am but I've got friends all over the place."

More muttering about lady cops, the general unfairness of the world and references to a particularly painful self-inflicted sex act, then in a small voice he said, "It wasn't really a robbery. It was more that I was hungry."

"Therefore a restaurant?"

"Right. I was hungry," he quickly agreed.

"You should keep your gloves on when you eat."

"Fingerprints?"

"Everywhere – on the fridge, on the ovens, on the cash register – odd place to keep food, don't you think? Robbery came to me because they ID'd your fingerprints in about ten minutes.

Two guys claimed they'd seen your prints so often they recognized them by sight."

"*Po gai! Po kai!!!*"

"I couldn't have said it better. But today's your lucky day. A little sand in a gas tank and all is forgiven."

"That simple, huh?"

"That simple."

And that simply she had her cover to get out of Hong Kong, or so she hoped.

At the entrance to the Nevada Texan strip club Joan tipped the doorman. The man pocketed the money, leered at her and said, "Dancin' tonight, honey?"

She smiled at him. He pulled aside the restraining rope and she entered the darkened club. The place had become even more popular since the arrival of the Beijing authority. The club and others like it represented an attachment to pleasure that was anathema to the puritanical Communists but was so much a part of the life of capitalist Hong Kongers. People now came to this club who wouldn't have been caught dead in a place like this just six years before.

Joan was directed to a small round table close to a corner, and before she smoothed out her skirt a martini was delivered. A demand for an outrageous amount of money quickly followed. Joan paid the tariff then asked, "Is Marie dancing tonight?" as she had been instructed to do in the Dalong Fada e-mail.

The waitress, a slender girl with better legs than brains, smiled and winked.

Joan assumed that meant yes.

Five minutes later a silicon wonder approached her table carrying a milk crate. "You been waiting all your life for me, sweetie?" the girl asked.

"Are you Marie?"

"No. Don't know any Maries."

Joan froze her out. "Get lost. And I'd be very careful with the breast augmentation. Latest studies have not been encouraging for the health of the recipient."

Ms. Silicon made a face. "Aren't you fun?" she said picking up her box and heading back into the darkness. On the stage, a dancer was removing a kimono, with surprising grace. She was not particularly beautiful but her control of the silk garment was alluring.

Joan spun as a hand landed on her shoulder. "I'm Marie. You asked for me?" The voice was deep, dusky. Joan went to turn but the voice commanded, "Don't." Joan looked straight ahead. "See the curtain on the far side to the left?" Joan was about to nod when she heard, "Don't move your head. When I'm finished, pay me, head toward the curtain and through it. Go down the corridor to the bathroom and out the window. There's a green Mini in the street at the end of the alley. The keys are beneath the driver's side floor mat. Instructions are in the glove compartment. Good luck. Now turn and give me a kiss like you mean it."

Joan turned her head and felt soft lips quickly press against hers. Then a silken tongue circled her teeth. She found herself responding. The face was too close to her for her to see it – that was the point. The dark voice said, "Don't respond. This isn't about sex. It's about the cause."

Then she was gone. Joan had no way to identify her if she were asked to. Which, once again, was the point. For an instant, Joan wondered at the complexity and professionalism of the system. Dalong Fada had only really been a presence for ten years and now it clearly had safe houses and methods that had been learned by the members.

A wave of fear washed over her. Then she remembered why she was doing what she was about to do. China needed an opposition and, at this point in time, only Dalong Fada could

stand in the way of the Beijing Communists destroying everything that Hong Kong had bled to build.

She dropped yet more cash on the small table, made as if
she was checking for something in her purse and headed
toward the curtain.

Getting through the curtain was much simpler than dealing
with the girls in the corridor on the other side of it. These girls
weren't paid to dance in the club. They paid the club to dance.
Their dancing was a live ad for services that they provided in
the dozens of small rooms that were on either side of the
lengthy corridor.

As Joan moved quickly down the corridor, the sounds and
sights of sex for cash presented themselves at nearly every
doorway. The positions varied but the basics of the transaction
were always the same – the girls serviced the customers
whether they were old or young, ugly or beautiful, men or
women.

Passing by one open door, Joan found herself momentarily
transfixed by the gaze of a naked whore perched on the edge of
the room's sink. In front of her, a young man on his knees had
buried his head between her thighs in what was clearly a vain
effort to bring this whore to the release of clouds and rain. From
the sounds emerging from her nether regions he was giving it
his best efforts. Lucky for him he couldn't see the look of infi-
nite boredom on the young woman's face.

That expression changed when she saw Joan in the doorway of her cubicle. A smile crossed her lips. Her hips began to
undulate against the young man's face as she mouthed the
words "Show me your tits" at Joan.

With the ease of a practiced "eloquent," Joan undid the top-
most button of her blouse, then the next down, then the next.
The whore's mouth went slack. Her eyes glazed over. "Good,"
Joan thought, "I want to be remembered as being here. I must

have been seen entering, might as well leave a real memory." As a cop she knew that this piece of information would be elicited early in the investigation and would stop everything else – hopefully long enough to let her get back from Shanghai and muddy the water with her Calden Inn alibi. Joan kept eye contact with the whore. The girl's eyes rolled back in her head and she let out a low sigh. Then she clamped her thighs tight to the young man's head and grabbed fistfuls of his thick black hair.

As soon as the whore's eyes closed, Joan raced to the bathroom at the end of the corridor. There were thankfully few people in her way and most were involved at the moment. She flung open the bathroom door, stood on the sink to reach the unlocked window, opened it and slipped out into the alley. The alley led her to a dimly lit street. There, across the roadway was the green Mini – unlocked, keys beneath the floor mat, instructions in the glove compartment and new identification papers affixed to the underside of the steering wheel.

She followed the directions to the ferry docks and guided her car into line for the next boat to the mainland. As the instructions directed, once she parked her car in the belly of the boat, she went up the bow stairway and entered the women's washroom. She counted four stalls, checked that the fourth was unused, then entered, closing but not locking the door behind her. The place wasn't overly clean but for a lavatory that serviced both Hong Kong and the mainland she'd expected much worse.

Five minutes later, the stall door was pushed open and a tiny, sharp-faced, older woman came in carrying a canvas bag. She didn't say a word but signalled Joan to sit on the toilet. There was no seat cover so Joan balanced on the rim. The tiny woman went behind her and sat on the toilet tank. From her bag she pulled out a pair of shears and began hacking away at Joan's long black hair. At first Joan wanted to resist then she said to herself, "Hey, it's only my hair." Then she said to herself, "Fuck, it's my hair." But she didn't say anything aloud. When most of her long hair was on the stall's floor, the woman hopped off the toilet tank and came around the front. She put a finger under Joan's chin and lifted it. Then she completed her work with smaller scissors.

When she finished cutting, she stood back and said her first words to Joan, "Take off your clothes." The first thought in Joan's head was that this was the only day in her life that two women had asked her to remove her clothing. She did as she was told.

The woman examined her naked body. But this was not the kind of examination that the whore would have done. This one was clearly critical and worried. The tiny woman reached into her bag and withdrew a large rolled tensor bandage and began to bind Joan's chest. "Let out your air." Joan did. A few minutes later, Joan's upper curves were flattened and uncomfortable. The tiny woman noticed and said, "Get used to it. Don't even think about taking it off until you're safely back in Hong Kong." Then a thought crossed the woman's face. As if the thought were somehow shouted aloud, Joan received the message crystal clear: After what you are going to do, even Hong Kong may not be safe.

The tiny woman took a tattered Mao jacket and the traditional pyjama-like leggings from her bag and held them out to Joan. Joan put them on. It was summer. The jacket was suffocatingly hot – and both the jacket and pants stunk. They were supposed to. She was a peasant. Peasants don't often smell nice.

"Take off your shoes," the woman ordered. When Joan did, the woman hissed in disapproval then slopped nail polish remover on Joan's toes, none too gently, wiped it off with a rag and slid on a pair of cheap sandals.

The woman then took a jar of theatrical "dirt" and rubbed wads of it into Joan's neck, hands, feet and forehead. Once rubbed in, it looked like stains not dirt, as if Joan had gone for many months without proper bathing.

"Hold out your hands." The woman examined them closely and shook her head. Joan used clear nail polish so that wasn't a problem but her nails were immaculate, a real source of pride for her. The woman took out her small scissors again and ripped at Joan's nails, purposefully slashing into her cuticles and cutting jaggedly wherever possible. Once that was done, she looked at a hanging section of nail on Joan's left ring finger and said, "Close your eyes. This might hurt." Before Joan could do as she was asked, the woman slipped the offending finger into her mouth, clamped on the hanging section with her teeth and gave a mighty yank with her head. The nail tore and half came out in the woman's mouth. She spat it to the ground. Joan felt as if she might faint. But she didn't.

The woman looked at Joan's hands and nodded. "Good. They might pass. Open your mouth." The woman took out a small vial with a dark liquid in it. Using a tiny brush she applied the liquid to several of Joan's teeth. "Tooth black," she explained as she put away the bottle. The woman then indicated that Joan should turn slowly. Joan did. The woman nodded, "As good as we can do for now." She reached into her pocket and held out a badly torn and aged identity card. Joan took it. The woman began to pack up, scooping large hunks of Joan's hair into her canvas bag. When she was done, she said, "Take five more minutes then come on deck."

"How will I know when five minutes is up? You have my watch."

"Count." The woman was clearly not impressed with Joan's first venture into peasanthood. "When you are on deck, don't sit. Don't look around. Get to the rail and stare at the water. When we land, you walk off. Give me the car keys and your other identity card."

Joan did.

"Good luck," the tiny woman said, "and if I was you I'd take a good dump here. It may be the last time you see a real toilet until you get back to Hong Kong."

When the ferry docked, Joan joined a long line of peasants who waited patiently while all the cars from below left the ferry, then the passengers in first class, second class and third class. Waiting without complaint was a new concept for Joan Shui.

At the bottom of the gangplank there was a government official backed by two armed guards demanding papers. When Joan's turn came, she held out her torn identity card. The man didn't even look at it as he barked, "Move along." This was new too. Not even a glance at her face, which was now dirt encrusted, or at her now seemingly non-existent chest, which thanks to the tensor bandage was beginning to really pinch.

She was used to being the object of much male and some female attention and for a moment it really threw her not to be thought of as attractive. Up until that moment she hadn't realized how much, in the past, she had relied on the unquestioned fact of her beauty. "*Sic transit gloria mundi*," she quoted to herself. A British education came in handy at the oddest of moments.

On the night train north, in the fourth-class hard-seat compartment, she met her land contact – she almost fell asleep against her shoulder before she knew. "Do the exercises in your mind, they'll keep you alert," the middle-aged woman whispered.

"I'm tired," Joan said but was immediately sorry that she had spoken. The man across the way had ferret eyes. He was a common reality in mainland China. He and the millions like him were the natural product of a system that didn't reward expertise but did reward those who rat on their fellow citizens. It was the only way that so few could control so many – Beijing had millions like this man working for them.

Joan fell back on instinct – charm your way out. Mistake! With her blackened teeth and cropped hair, her smile and head bob were hardly fetching. His response shocked her. "An ugly whore," he shouted. "What's an ugly whore doing on the same train with honest comrades?"

That was enough. Joan swallowed some air, as her younger brother had taught her to do many years ago at a family gathering, and belched right in the man's face.

He spat on the floor at her feet. She spat at his feet.

He stared at her. She stared right back.

They made quite a pair.

Despite the fact that the train actually did go all the way to Shanghai, Joan and her escort got off as the sun was rising, some 200 miles south of the great city.

"This train comes in to the North Train Station in Shanghai. It is watched. Always watched," her escort said ominously. Once off the train, the heat hit Joan like a moist blanket. At least on the train there had been the motion of air through the windows. But here the air just hung from the dawning sky like a living, sleeping thing. Joan reached to undo the top buttons of her Mao jacket. "Don't," the woman said, "peasants are very wary of showing their bodies."

Joan took her hands away from the buttons. "These sandals cut my feet."

"Good," said the woman as they left the train station and headed toward the old section of the small city.

CHAPTER NINE

COUNTERWEIGHTS

As the heat of the day began to mount, Fong and Chen climbed up on the stage. Behind them, several other cops lugged a large black bag into the auditorium.

"What now?" demanded the old worker from the far reaches upstage.

"Thanks for joining us," said Fong in an effort to calm the waves of open aggression coming from the man.

The old worker looked at Fong then did a double take as he glanced at Chen. Chen was used to that. "What do you and your intensely ugly friend want?"

Fong started to defend Chen, but the younger man spoke first, "You work the fly rail here?"

"Some nights," the old worker replied warily.

"Which nights?" asked Fong.

"Whichever they assign me. What is this? I was told I had to work on this shit. I don't know squat about it. It's ridiculous. I'm a rigger. A professional, not some stupid rope puller. I worked on skyscrapers in the Pudong then all of a sudden I'm told to go pull ropes for faggots. What's that?"

"These ropes that you pull, they are all your responsibility?"

"Yeah, there are seven sets of lines and they are all mine to work – on the nights I have to waste my time here."

"And each of the ropes . . . "

"Lines. They're called lines."

"Okay each of the lines has counterweights on them?"

"Naturally. Some of the flying units weigh close to half a ton. Without counterweights no one could lower the thing in without smashing it to the ground, let alone fly it out."

"Yeah, I get that, but whose responsibility is it to set the counterweights?"

"Mine . . . for the . . . "

" . . . nights you waste your time and talent here. Right. So this was the line Geoffrey Hyland was hanged from?"

"Who?"

"The director who was hanged. You may recall that incident."

"Yeah. It was tied off to the pinrail when I arrived that morning."

"How much counterweight was there on that line?"

"A lot."

"More than usually is on the line?"

"Way more."

"Do you know how much more?"

"I'm a professional, of course I know how much weight was . . . "

"How much?"

The man went into the small production office in the back and came out with a well-kept leather-bound notebook. He turned to the date and pointed to a figure. The man's handwriting was like a draftsman's. The columns were perfectly in line. The whole thing was a work of mathematical precision. Fong looked at the man. Perhaps his talents were, in fact, wasted here.

"So there were three hundred and forty pounds of counterweight on that line that night?"

"That's what it says, so that's what was there."

Fong nodded. "How much does that line usually carry?"

The man checked his notes. "Forty pounds when I work it and sixty when the other guy does."

"Because . . . ?" Fong prompted.

"Because I'm stronger than the other guy who isn't a guy at all but an old woman who needs the extra counterweight to move the damn thing."

"What do you pull up and down on this line?"

"You mean what's flown in and out on this line?"

"Yes, I guess I mean that."

"Several vertical white panels. Used for the ghost's appearance in the bedroom and for Ophelia's madness walk with the flowers."

"Just canvas panels?"

"That's it. Pretty light but that director was very specific about how he wanted the panels flown in and out. It was in time to this real slow music so we needed enough counterweight to make the move smooth. When it worked it was . . . good, you know."

Fong nodded. Even this resentful old man saw the beauty in Geoff's work. "Where are the counterweights kept?" He pointed to four stacks of iron weights on a rolling cart upstage of the last pinrail line. Fong thanked him for his help. "Just one more thing."

"What?"

"Did actors use the chair that was here?"

"There's not supposed to be any chair here."

"No?"

"No. I wouldn't allow actors here. This is my territory and I'm . . . "

"A professional, you've told us already."

"Yeah. And I wouldn't use a chair because it was my job to be ready." He was clearly about to reiterate that he was a professional but decided against it. He just harrumphed. Then he said, "Anything else?"

"No. Thanks again for your help."

As the man left, Chen went to get the counterweights, and four cops shut the various doors to the theatre and then stood by. The rest of the cops muscled the black bag onto the stage and cracked it open. First, they took out a duplicate of the noose that had suffocated Geoffrey Hyland. Then they propped up a mannequin weighted to be just under a hundred and eighty pounds. Geoff's weight.

Fong walked the stage floor while, with the use of ladders, the noose was threaded through the pulleys and then brought down to the pinrail stage left. Then Chen added 340 pounds of counterweight to the flyline.

The mannequin was set centre stage and the noose put around its neck. "Captain Chen, are you ready?"

"Yes," said Chen as he took up a position by the pinrail.

"Now, unloop the line and pull."

Chen untied the line and gave it a yank. The mannequin rose easily off the stage toward the fly gallery. The cops were impressed. Fong signalled Chen to drop the line back in. He did and the mannequin slid gracefully to the stage. "Do it harder, Chen."

Chen did and the mannequin moved faster toward the fly gallery. "Let it back down, Chen." The dummy moved smoothly back to the stage. "Now do it hand over hand as fast as you can?"

Chen did and the mannequin moved rapidly all the way up to the fly gallery and stayed there.

Fong shook his head and began to pace. Chen approached him. "It works, sir. With the counterweights, the murderer didn't need to get Mr. Hyland to climb the ladder. So it answers that question, doesn't it?"

"That question, perhaps, Captain Chen."

"But it shows how someone could have hanged Mr. Hyland."

"Partly."

"Why partly? The counterweights make it easy enough to lift him."

"Fine, Chen, but how did they get the noose around his neck? He wasn't drugged. Even if you could get the noose around his neck, how do you stop him from taking it off if he's in the centre of the stage and you are all the way over stage left at the pinrail?" Then Fong stopped and looked at the scuffmark on the stage-right proscenium arch. He flipped open his cell phone and punched the speed dial for Forensics. "Lily, have you done the paint match yet?"

"Yes. Very simple. The paint on the arch and Mr. Hyland's shoe match."

"Thanks, Lily," Fong said and snapped shut his phone.

Fong took off his right shoe and tossed it to a cop standing by the pinrail door. "Smear mud on that." The man was about to ask why then thought better of it when he saw the set of Fong's jaw. Moments later, he returned and gave Fong his now muddy shoe. Fong took the shoe and put it on the mannequin's right foot, lacing it up, careful not to get mud on his hands. "Bring the mannequin over beside you at the pinrail, Captain Chen." He did. "Now put the noose around its neck. You'll have to let in more line to do it."

Fong closed his eyes for a moment. A new horrific image was ready to force its way into the sack around his heart, increasing the ghostly weight yet again.

"It's ready, sir," said Chen

"Now pull hard, hand over hand."

Fong hopped down off the stage and headed to the back of the auditorium.

"Ready, sir?" Chen called out.

Fong didn't turn around; he didn't have to. "Yes, Chen. I'm

ready." Fong knew exactly what would happen.

The mannequin rose out of stage left in a large arch, flew across the stage like the base of a pendulum. The mannequin's right shoe hit just above the scuffmark on the stage-right proscenium, leaving a muddy slash, and then the mannequin swung obscenely back and forth as it was hauled to its resting place just below the centre of the proscenium arch.

Chen was ecstatic. "Right. Perfect . . . " But he stopped before he completed his thought.

Fong had left the theatre. He now knew two things for sure that he'd been uncertain of before. He knew that it was possible to hang Geoff and that Geoff's hanging was the work of at least two people: one to put the noose around Geoff's neck, one to pull the counterweighted flyline.

Sometimes knowledge sets you free. Sometimes it makes you want to puke.

Standing in the shadows at the back of the auditorium, Li Chou didn't want to puke. He wanted to jump for joy. He already had motive: jealousy – and now he had means: counterweights. All he needed was opportunity.

As the men packed up the equipment, Captain Chen found Fong outside the theatre. "That leads to something else, doesn't it, sir?"

Fong nodded. "My place is just around the corner. Let's talk there."

Once in Fong's rooms, Chen didn't know where to look. His wife, Lily, had lived here with Fong. The shadowed outline of the antique lintel piece she had bought that caused so much trouble was still on the wall beside the window.

A letter from the condo people awaited Fong on the floor just inside the door. He opened it and was informed that he had only two weeks left "to make his intentions known." It went on to suggest to him that an "insider's price" like this was a once-in-a-lifetime thing. Ignoring Chen, Fong went into the bedroom and put the "offer sheet" on his desk. So much money to buy what was already his. When had this place that he and Fu Tsong had loved in stopped being his? When had it become theirs? Whoever they were. He remembered the French guys with blueprints and "bum-winged" silk jackets and their Beijing keeper with the raspberry-stained cheek.

So they were the ones who offered him the special insider's price. And what a price! He moved the offer sheet to the top-left corner of his desk. Then to the top-right corner. Then to the centre – yep, everywhere he put the thing, the price was still completely beyond his means, way beyond. The only people he knew who had this kind of money were people he had arrested and were now spending time in jail. How could anyone, anywhere, make this kind of money, let alone have it just lying around to spend on buying back something that was already theirs?

Finally he made a decision. He folded the damn thing and shoved it in the desk drawer. That felt better. Then he remembered that Chen was waiting for him in the other room. When he entered, Chen was looking out the window at the courtyard with the ludicrous Henry Moore–esque statue in it. "Tea, Captain Chen?"

Chen nodded and Fong poured hot water from a large Thermos he kept on the floor into a simple ceramic teapot. "So this was definitely a murder then, sir?" asked Chen bluntly.

"A murder made to look like a suicide," said Fong as he swirled the water around inside the pot to get the tea to infuse the liquid.

"Then shouldn't we start with opportunity, sir?" asked Captain Chen.

Fong noted the strength in Chen's voice, wondered about it for a moment then nodded. He poured the hot liquid into a clean jelly jar and held it out to Chen.

The man didn't take the proffered *cha*. "Keys for the theatre then? Isn't that where we should start? Who had keys to get into the theatre. Keys provide opportunity. Opportunity is the place we should start."

Fong nodded. Chen took the *cha*. Fong hesitated. Suddenly new vistas of danger were opening as this very sturdy, very dogged cop stood before him drinking his tea. "Let's get a list of those who have keys to the theatre, Chen."

"Shouldn't the custodian have a list, sir?"

Fong thought of saying that he would pick up the list then put that idea aside. He would just have to weather the storm that list would let loose.

"Surely he'd know who has keys," said Chen.

Again Fong nodded – that old man knew. He knew too much.

The old geezer rummaged through a stack of papers on the floor and mumbled angrily. Chen stood patiently waiting for the standard Shanghanese complaints about authority to run their course. They finally did. "Keys? It's keys you want? To the theatre?"

"No," Chen almost shouted. The man was clearly hard of hearing but it was also possible that he was delaying for some reason. "I want to know who has keys to the theatre."

Then the man brightened and pushed aside a desk to get at an old filing cabinet. He opened it by twisting the handle and giving it two sharp knocks to the side – your basic Soviet-made locking mechanism. The cabinet, surprisingly, had only one tall drawer. The old man took out several large, mounted, theatre posters and dropped them onto the desk with a thud.

The poster on top featured a lithograph of a profoundly beautiful actress. Chen read the information. The play was by an English playwright whose name he didn't recognize. But the name of the actress was extremely familiar – Fu Tsong. Chen looked at the image, the exquisite skin, the deep deep eyes, and marvelled.

"She was more than just a looker," said the old custodian. "She made birds sing in the trees when she acted. I never missed a performance when she was acting. And her Peking Opera work was . . . " Unable to find the words, he waved his liver-spotted hands like a fan in front of his face. Then he smiled unabashedly showing off an almost toothless maw.

"Have you found the list of theatre keyholders?"

"Yep," the man replied and handed over a much-rumpled pad of paper and then returned to admiring Fu Tsong's likeness.

Chen read the handwritten list on the top page. Names were printed, then a signature appeared beside each name. Chen assumed you signed out the keys. The list was predictable: Mr. Hyland as director had one, as did his two Canadian producers, as did the old man in front of him – those names were expected. Chen flipped through the following pages. Each entry was signed and then crossed off when the key was returned. Nineteen pages later he saw the first entry that had not been crossed off. The name there was Zhong Fong.

Back in Fong's office on the Bund, Chen reported most of his findings.

"I'll want to interview each of the keyholders at the office. Out of courtesy we'll see the custodian in his room."

"No need, sir. He gave me an alibi for the time in question and it checks out." Now it was Chen who hesitated.

Fong stood. "There were more keyholders?"

Captain Chen nodded.

"Tell me," said Fong knowing full well his name and signature ought to be on the list.

"You're the only other name on the list, sir."

Fong nodded. "Want my alibi, Captain Chen?"

Captain Chen looked past Fong, out the window, to the Bund. Fong felt for the young man, trapped between his admiration for him and his need to do the right thing. Fong sighed. "I took Xiao Ming to the theatre and brought her back to you and Lily by 10:30 p.m. The rest of the night I was home. Alone. Reading. Not much of an alibi is it?"

Chen didn't meet Fong's eyes.

Fong took a step toward Chen. The younger man backed away. "I've told you that this is a political place. You must protect yourself in a situation like this, Captain Chen." The country cop nodded and finally met Fong's eyes. "Tell the next in command about my name on the list then arrange for me to interrogate the other keyholders."

Captain Chen bore the brunt of much mockery from Li Chou and his men. But this afternoon they were not busy thinking up nasty cracks about his appearance. This time they offered him a seat and listened carefully to his story about theatre keys, keyholders and Zhong Fong.

Li Chou had to stop himself from chuckling and rubbing his chubby hands together as he closed his office door behind Chen. All would be inappropriate under the circumstances but all were burbling up inside him. Motive – jealousy; means – counterweights that Fong had deviously pointed out to all and sundry; opportunity – Fong lived literally two minutes away from the theatre because his wife had been a star there and he had a key. His name and signature were on the caretaker's list.

A knock at his door. "The commissioner wants to see you in his office now, sir."

Li Chou nodded. Of course he does. After the report he put on the man's desk about Fong's history with the dead Westerner, what else could he possibly want?

Li Chou stood up and did his best to straighten his jacket. His weight was beginning to show. "That damned cheese my wife likes so much," he thought. It never occurred to him that he was not being force-fed the Western-style sweet dairy confection. Be that as it may, he now had girth where there did not used to be girth.

"I want Chen followed," he said to his men. "He may lead us to even more interesting information."

This was a good day. A very good day. Passing by Fong's office, he nigh on clicked his heels and Shrug and Knock smiled broadly. But when he got to the commissioner's office, his joyful bubble burst all over his puffed-out chest.

"This report is garbage. Nothing more than speculation. Why are you wasting your time on this?"

Li Chou couldn't believe it. He was sure that the commissioner was as anxious to rid the police force of Zhong Fong as he was. Here was the perfect opportunity and the man was letting it pass by. Why?

"Have you shared this with your men?"

"No, sir," he lied.

"Good. Don't. And that's an order." The commissioner slid Li Chou's report into the shredder beside his desk and flipped a switch. A brief electric humming followed and shortly thereafter Fong's comeuppance was little more than strips of indecipherable text.

But why? Then Li Chou looked at the commissioner's desk. There had always been two phones there – one internal, one external. But now there was a third phone that had no keypad. A direct line, no doubt scrambled. Such things in the People's Republic of China only went to one place – Beijing. Li Chou covered his new knowledge with a smile and backed out of the commissioner's office. So there was more to this than Li Chou had first seen. Fine. But was that to Li Chou's advantage or not?

An hour later, there was a light tapping on Fong's office door. "It's open."

The door swung open slowly revealing the figure of Shrug and Knock leaning against the door jamb. "There's a really white Long Nose here who says he needs to speak with you. Or at least I think that's what he's trying to say. His Mandarin is awful."

"Take a name and get his phone number and tell him I'll get back to him," said Fong, returning to the dossiers on his desk.

"Fine," said Shrug and Knock as he closed Fong's office door.

Two minutes later, he returned with a baby-blue-and-yellow business card and a small oblong leather case. "He said to give these to you. Something about he was concerned you were going to bump into things without them."

Fong looked at the business card with the sickening colours – he'd seen more attractive baby puke – and couldn't help but smile. Dr. Morris Wasniachenko – the Ukrainian optometrist. Then he flipped open the small leather case. What he saw there took the smile from his face. Eyeglasses.

More proof that he was getting old.

"Nice," said Shrug and Knock with a big smile. "Oh, yeah, I almost forgot, your 'interrogatees' are here. The people who had keys, those who were last in the theatre and those coming to rehearsal are ready for you, as you wanted, Detective Zhong."

Fong nodded then indicated that Shrug and Knock should close the door.

Fong slid the glasses out of their case and put them on. They made a difference. He caught a reflection of himself in his office window. He didn't like what he saw. He took off the glasses and slid them into his pocket.

He looked again at the dossiers of the "interrogatees." He really didn't think these folks were very promising suspects. Geoff's death smacked of real intricacy. Something that linked more logically to his Beijing keepers and what they wanted him to find in Geoff's room. But he hadn't found anything of any particular interest. He loosened the tension in his shoulders and read through his notes on the people waiting for him in the various interrogation rooms around the station one more time.

An hour later, he realized that he hadn't heard from Captain Chen since he reported his key findings to Li Chou. When he contacted the front desk, he was told Captain Chen had booked off sick. Fong didn't like it but he put it aside and completed his preparations for the interrogations.

CHAPTER TEN

THE INTERROGATEES

The young man playing Hamlet was, well, young. And vacuous and "really sorry that Mr. Hyland was gone." The man was so wrapped up in himself that Fong cut him short with a demand for an alibi for the night of the murder. The young man supplied both the name of an all-night dance club and those of five of his dance partners. For a second time Fong noted that the man looked like a younger Chinese version of Geoff but there was nothing in Hamlet's words or actions that was even remotely revealing. Fong ended the interrogation early. After all, how many times could he hear "What am I going to do without him, you know, like, what am I going to do?"

Fong's second interrogation was more complicated. Hao Yong had been an admirer of his wife and for a very brief time had been Geoff's lover. "I was young but not a child. I take full responsibility for my actions. I am sure that I gained more from our relationship than he did. The time we spent together was very important to me both as a person and as an artist."

"Do you still . . . "

"See Mr. Hyland? Only professionally. I would work for him at any time . . . " then she stopped herself, evidently realizing for the first time that she would never again be guided through a play by Geoff.

Fong surprised himself with his next question. "Was Geoff sad or upset?"

"The Screaming me-me's got to him."

"The who?"

"The me-me's are what Geoff called the two Canadian lady producers."

Fong nodded, "I've met them."

She nodded back and a gentle smile creased her lips for a moment. Then she bowed her head. Fong thought she might cry. But she didn't. She raised her head. Her eyes glistened. "Detective Zhong, if you could go through your loss and not take your life, what could possibly cause Mr. Hyland to take his?"

"But Geoff did not take his own life," Fong thought.

She stood. "Anything else, Detective Zhong?" she asked.

"Was Geoff 'seeing' anyone this time?" He knew the question would hurt Hao Yong and he had no desire to inflict any pain on her but he needed to know.

"I am a married woman, Detective Zhong, with a baby girl. I mind my own business and do my own work so I would not know the answer to your question."

After a sigh, he requested her alibi. She supplied her husband's phone number to corroborate her story, turned and left the room.

Fong felt her absence the moment the door closed behind her. "Artists do that," he thought, "leave a room wanting when they leave."

The third interrogation was with the actor playing Horatio. The young man was clearly conflicted. He thought Geoff was an extraordinary artist and was thrilled to work with him but was angered that he had been consigned to playing what he called "Hamlet's best bud." "There's just not a lot of latitude in the role and I really wanted to show Mr. Hyland my stuff. He's amazing. Have you seen the show? Look what he can do." He stopped himself, realizing that he was speaking of Geoff in the wrong tense.

Then suddenly he was speaking very loudly. "Why him, Detective Zhong? There are hundreds, maybe thousands of awful directors. Power-mad maniacs who don't know anything. Then there was Geoff. You know what I mean?" Fong did but he dodged the question then requested and received a substantial alibi for the hours in question. He took his leave of the young actor and headed to the next room.

The interview with Da Wei, Geoff's homely translator, yielded even less than the previous three. It began with Da Wei crying, continued with her in tears and ended with her sobbing, "He gave us so much." Fong got an address from her and told her, "I'll see you later when you've calmed down a bit."

The actors playing Ophelia and Laertes sat side by side as Fong entered their interrogation room. They were an attractive young couple. Her long hair was held back by a large clip. She had the gentle softness that made some Asian beauty so unique. She also had a deep sadness in her eyes. Fu Tsong had done a lot of talking about eyes. "We wear our history in our eyes, Fong. All our joys and troubles are there. It's why so many women have sad eyes. But as an actress I must not let the audience see my eyes first. I must make them see my mouth, then my eyes."

"You have sad eyes," he'd said.

She had smiled and said, "I have earned my sad eyes, Husband."

"But your sad eyes don't make you a sad person," he'd replied.

"You would think I was a sad person if I let you see them first. Instead I drop my sense of myself down to my mouth. You look there first and then, only after acknowledging me as Fu Tsong, do you notice that my eyes are sad. It is then that they become beautiful because they sit in opposition to what you see when I make you deal with my face from the mouth up. Besides, there are three positions to wear your eyes."

"Wear your eyes?"

"Yes, that is the right phrase, Husband, wear your eyes. You can make them hard where they become mirrors. Most people have lots of practice doing this since they have been in boring school forever and they do that hard-eyed thing to give off the international signal for 'I'm not sleeping, heck no, I'm listening.'" He'd laughed at her impersonation. "Or you can wear your eyes soft where they become, as Mr. Shakespeare says, the windows of the soul, or you can retract them – sit behind them if you wish. It is the place of waiting or watching. It is a wary place, a dangerous place."

" You can do that? Really?"

"Really, Husband." And then she'd done one of each "wearing position" in such quick but accurate succession that he began to laugh. "What?" she'd demanded.

"Well, which one are you?"

"This one," she said and softened her eyes that made his eyes drop to her mouth. Her gentle beauty overwhelmed him. Then he noted the sadness in her eyes, which so perfectly contrasted with the strength of her face that he smiled.

"You are very beautiful," he'd said.

She had not responded, just removed her gown and slipped into bed and nestled into his side.

He smiled, then noticed that Ophelia and Laertes were looking at him. He wondered for a moment if he'd said any of this out loud. From the looks on their faces, evidently not. Just taken a very long pause. He continued the pause and looked carefully at Laertes. He was not as attractive and a bit older than his Ophelia and he sat behind his eyes – in the place of waiting and watching. As Fu Tsong had said, a wary place.

Laertes leaned forward in his chair. His eyes softened as he said, "Mr. Hyland's death has touched us all."

Fong looked at the young couple. They held hands. She leaned against his shoulder. Then Ophelia began to cry.

Fong had had quite enough of women crying and snapped at Laertes, "I'll be next door. When your friend has regained her composure, tell the guard outside and he'll get me."

In the next interrogation room Fong found another couple holding hands. Both were male this time. The actor playing Guildenstern interlocked his fingers with Rosencrantz's beautifully manicured ones. Gay men were nothing new to Fong. Through Fu Tsong he had many contacts in the gay community and had, more than once, come to the rescue of a gay couple who had found themselves in trouble with the puritanical Communist authorities.

Fong looked at Guildenstern. The man withdrew his hand from his partner. "Detective Zhong, how can we help?"

Fong turned his head to one side. He wondered if Guildenstern knew that the offer to "help" was often seen as a sign of potential guilt.

"I'm not sure."

"We'll help in any way we can. What happened to Geoffrey is just terrible. Terrible. A great loss."

Fong looked to Rosencrantz. "How did you get along with Mr. Hyland?"

"As a director or as a person?" Rosencrantz asked.

Fong momentarily wondered if there was a person Geoffrey Hyland different from the director Geoffrey Hyland. He thought not but answered, "As a director."

"He was great if he liked you."

"Liked you or liked your work?"

"What's the difference?" Rosencrantz asked.

Fong wasn't sure about that either so he chose one, "Liked your work."

"He rode my case pretty hard but I liked him. He had standards and wanted them met without excuse."

That sounded right to Fong. He turned to Guildenstern. "How did you get along with Mr. Hyland?"

"He liked me. So I liked him." The man shrugged his slender shoulders. "That's how the world works, isn't it?"

Fong thought about that for a moment then asked where the two of them were last night. "There was a party," said Rosencrantz.

Guildenstern shot him a look.

"I'm with Special Investigations, not Vice."

Rosencrantz supplied the information about the party and the phone numbers of some people who were there. As he finished he let out a sigh.

"What?" Fong demanded.

Rosencrantz looked to Guildenstern who nodded. "There were party members at the party, if you get my meaning." Fong got his meaning and wasn't surprised. The party may have a puritanical face but behind closed doors sex was sex. To many it gave meaning to life. At very least it held death at bay – for however brief an instant.

The guard knocked at the door. "Has she stopped crying?" asked Fong.

"Who can tell with actresses?" the guard replied.

Fong let that pass and headed back to Laertes and Ophelia. Ophelia's tears had disturbed her carefully applied makeup. A slender line of black marked her left cheek.

"Feeling better?" he asked.

"A little, thank you, Detective."

That sounded honest enough. He turned to Laertes. "I hear

that Mr. Hyland could be very hard on actors. How did he treat you?"

"He hated me," said Laertes, "as if it were my fault the guy he cast as Hamlet couldn't cut it."

Fong recalled Laertes' attack on Hamlet with the fight master and smiled – so that was what that was all about – just your basic theatre scrap over casting. Would someone murder over casting? Fong doubted it. If so, why didn't he murder the guy playing Hamlet?

He turned to Ophelia, "And you?"

"He liked me. He liked my acting." She reached up and unclipped her hair.

The interrogation didn't seem to be going anywhere. They were each other's alibis claiming that they spent the night together. Fong made a note to check with the house warden although he knew that the warden system at the Shanghai Theatre Academy was as weak as the key-lady system in guest-houses. He reminded them that this was a murder investigation and that they were not to leave the city without his permission. He demanded their passports but neither had one since neither had ever left the People's Republic of China.

At the door he looked back at them. She rested her head against his shoulder, her long hair, loose from its clip, fell to the floor, revealing the nape of her neck. Laertes spoke to her softly, reassuringly. She tilted her head to accept his kiss. They were an attractive young couple. The kiss was tender, sweet.

Fong snapped shut his folder on Ms. Kitty Pants, the smaller of Geoff's Screaming me-me's, as the woman strode into his office. He didn't stand. She didn't sit. "Thank you for coming," Fong began.

"You summoned me, I didn't come because I wanted to. I have a show that I have to get ready."

"Really?"

"Really." She clutched her red zippered binder tightly to her chest and actually tapped her little foot.

Fong went through his mental file on North Americans and really didn't think he'd met one like Kitty Pants before. Through Fu Tsong he had met several American producers but Ms. Pants wasn't like them. She had their swagger but not their style. In fact, her style reminded him more of a petty bureaucrat at a post office checking foreign packages for correct "stampage," if there is such a word. Was it possible she was some sort of government producer? Was there such a thing? Fong did recall Geoff bemoaning the state of his country's arts that were as he put it "in the hands of people who can write grants to people who have written grants. Fifty-year-old failed women who have control over artists and not a clue what art is – I like to think of them as me-me's." Fong looked at the woman – one of Geoff's me-me's. She sat. Now that he hadn't asked her to sit, naturally she sat. Was she always so angry and officious he wondered, or was this an act she reserved for him?

"What's in the book?"

"It's not a book, it's a binder."

"Fine. What's in the binder, Ms. Pants?"

"My notes on the show. I never let them out of my sight."

"Do you take many notes?"

"More than Mr. Hyland ever did. They're my record of how we got to where we got and they never . . . "

"Leave your sight. You mentioned that already. Now who makes the rehearsal schedule?"

"Nominally, Geoff."

"Nominally?"

"Well, he makes requests and I sort out the problems he creates."

"Geoff creates problems?"

"He's disorganized. He's impulsive. He's . . . "

"An artist," Fong wanted to complete her thought but decided not to. Instead he said, "You didn't like Mr. Hyland?"

"Oh, I liked him fine, but he was a director in desperate need of someone like me who could harness his energies in the proper fashion."

Fong had seen several of Geoff's previous productions at the theatre academy. All had been excellent and none of them had needed a person like Kitty Pants to help him harness his energies. Geoff had, in fact, worked totally on his own, often using no one but his translator Da Wei to assist him. Again Fong looked at this woman. Was this a unique product of Canada – like a moose? Then he reminded himself that people were people. If it looked like a squid and swam like a squid and inked like a squid – it was a squid, whether an Asian or a Caucasian squid made no difference. He'd seen lots of Asians like this before. He nodded. What sat in front of him was just an angry control freak, filled with her own self-importance. He'd also seen lots of these folks before. He pressed a button on his desk and spoke quickly into the intercom in Mandarin, confident that Ms. Pants didn't speak a word of the Common Tongue. Chen answered.

"Sir?"

"I thought you were sick?"

"I was but I'm better."

Fong let that hang for a moment then said, "Good, come into the office and demand in Mandarin that Ms. Pants get up, then demand that she walk over and stand in the corner with her face to the wall." Chen's chuckle began to erupt from the box but Fong clicked it off before it hit the air.

"Planning some outrage, are we?" Ms. Pants asked with feigned casualness.

Fong just smiled. "Just one more question."

"If you have to."

"I do. There is a dead man – you may recall that."

That sobered her up a little. "Rehearsal was to begin at ten o'clock, right?"

"Right. It should have been nine o'clock but Geoff was such a lazy . . . "

"Right," he said snapping her off. "And did Geoff make the schedule that called Laertes and Ophelia in first, or did you?"

"He did. I tried to talk him out of it but . . . "

Chen entered the room without knocking and indicated that Ms. Pants should stand up. She looked to Fong, who shrugged his shoulders with his best it's-a-Communist-country-what-can-I-do look. Then Chen pointed her to the corner of the room and barked a country nursery rhyme in Mandarin. She went to the corner then Chen indicated with his finger that she should turn around and face the wall. He barked the nursery rhyme again but backwards this time. She resisted, but Chen screamed the opening lines of Mao's red book at her.

Captain Chen was having fun.

Ms. Pants finally turned around and faced the wall still clutching her red zippered binder with the ever-so-valuable insights on the show's progress.

Fong smiled then the two of them left the office and quietly shut the door. Once they were outside Chen asked, "Is she a suspect?"

"Of what?"

"Mr. Hyland's murder?"

"No."

"So what is she suspected of doing?"

A person like Ms. Pants, Fong assumed, could have organized a killing and staged it to look like a suicide but he couldn't for the life of him think what her motive for doing so would be. Besides, the whole thing had artistic touches. The way Geoff was dressed, the positioning of the ladder, the flowers – artistic. And this woman didn't have an artistic bone in her tight-assed body. "She's suspected of being offensive to art. And of bad manners."

Chen just stared at Fong. Fong pointed toward the room. "Get her passport then let her go."

Chen turned to the office then stopped. "I don't speak English."

"No, you don't." Fong smiled. "Just keep yelling in Mandarin until she figures it out. It's good for a person like her to feel powerless. It's what she enjoys doing to others. Maybe it will make her think twice before acting that way. Then again maybe it won't." Fong turned on his heel and headed toward the interrogation room the cops nicknamed the Hilton because it had a chair with all four legs and had been cleaned at least once in the past fiscal year.

The other Screaming me-me, Ms. Marstal, sat looking as if her hands needed a cigarette. She didn't stand when Fong entered but that was okay. Fong moved to the far side of the table and sat. He opened a folio and quickly leafed through the pages despite the fact that he already knew all the data there by heart.

"So you are here as an adviser to the production?"

"That's not how I would describe it."

That surprised Fong. "How would you describe it then?"

"My ex-husband put up the money for this. We were going to try out the concepts that Mr. Hyland had over here. Don't ask me how Geoff talked my ex into doing it in Shanghai. If he wanted out of town we could have done New Haven or something."

Fong nodded although he had no idea what she was talking about. "Your money was behind the production?"

"Yes. My ex-husband's."

"Didn't the theatre academy produce the show?"

"They gave us the space and actors . . . "

"That's not producing a show?"

"Well, if you count that, I guess it was, but really the actors here . . . " She didn't complete her thought.

Fong knew that Geoff was able to attract the finest actors in China. "You had a problem with some of the actors?"

"Not a problem, they just aren't very talented."

"Really?"

"Especially the poor thing playing Gertrude."

Fong stopped listening as Ms. Marstal slandered Hao Yong's work in the play. Fong understood what this was all about and began to nod and smile.

"Something funny, Detective?"

"Inspector."

"Fine. Inspector, what is so humorous?"

Fong took a breath and remembered Fu Tsong's comments about actresses who married rich producers. "They deprecate and fawn, Fong, and continually try to prove they haven't slept their way into their roles. They usually have good tits but not enough brains to do the work. They always get attracted to the ethereal side of acting. There is real magic in good acting, Husband, but not the way their small brains can comprehend."

When he looked up, Ms. Marstal was talking again.

"Geoff is so didactic – I'm interested in the spontaneous – channelling is the height of the form." Then she laughed. Fong assumed she did that because she thought he didn't understand what the hell she was talking about. He did – joke on you, lady. Then she rose and sort of posed against the door jamb, "Geoff didn't find me attractive." She waited for Fong to contradict Geoff's taste. He didn't. Finally she unfurled herself from the door and said, "Fool, him."

Fong wanted to say, "Geoff chased skirts not rags," but thought better of it. Then he remembered the rest of that conversation with Fu Tsong about actresses like Ms. Marstal. "And then when they get older they use phrases like 'old dames like me' or 'has-beens like me,' but never believe them, Fong. They think they are still sixteen and want to be treated as if they hold the key to the secret gates to ecstasy all by themselves."

"Ms. Marstal, is it hard to find work at your age?"

"Excuse me?" she said, clearly caught off balance by Fong's question.

"I believe you heard me. It must be difficult for an actress of your age in a field so dedicated to youth."

She softened. "Well, it's hard for old dames like me, yes."

"And Gertrude was your role to play once the show moved back to North America?"

"Yes. How did you know?"

Fong just smiled. "Why were you at the theatre for a ten o'clock call?"

"I attend most rehearsals."

"But no Gertrude scene was called."

"True, but Geoff needed guidance. I noticed him moving the show in a most unacceptable way."

"What way was that?"

"Conceptual. As if his concept were more important than the actors."

"And that didn't suit the show?"

"No. It almost entirely undermines Gertrude's character." Fong smiled again and nodded. Ms. Marstal saw it and wasn't pleased. "Gertrude is Hamlet's mother. Her story is central to the whole thing. And she's a sexually alive human being. She's the sexual centre of the play itself." She did that smiley thing again and said, "I mean how many times do has-beens like me get a chance to strut our stuff? I was at rehearsal to protect my role. If you knew anything about actresses you would understand my position."

Fong let that pass. "So what happens now?"

"Meaning . . . ?"

"Who looks after the show after Geoff is gone?"

"That duty falls to me. I've always wanted to direct. If I

weren't a woman I would have been asked to do so years ago. Did you know that Elinora Duza played Hamlet?"

No, Fong didn't know that. Nor did he know what an Elinora Duza was – perhaps some form of puffy Italian pastry or maybe it was the name for a Big Whopper in Rome or something. What he did know was that this woman wasn't smart enough to plan the demise of Geoffrey Hyland. And even getting a chance to direct was not motive enough for murder. If, through some bizarre alignment of the stars or some trick of alchemy, the killing of a talented director would revive the career of a mediocre actress then Fong would have arrested Ms. Marstal on the spot. But since there wasn't a hope of any such extraterritorial happenings he unceremoniously demanded her passport and left her to find her own way out of the police station.

It was already dark as Fong entered his office. He sat at his desk and thought, "So much for the keyholders and those who were in the theatre just before and those called to be in the theatre just after Geoff's death." He slid the dossiers into a desk drawer. Then he noticed a piece of paper with a phone number on it. Beneath the number was Chen's notation: *Shakespeare Expert.*

He looked at the clock on the wall. Enough for today. He picked up the piece of paper and turned off the lights in his office. Standing in the dark, he looked at the dancing neon of the nighttime Pudong across the Huangpo River. Every day it seemed to grow.

He left the office, putting the phone number on Shrug and Knock's desk with a note attached to it saying "I want him in my office first thing tomorrow morning."

The office was almost deserted. He headed down the back stairway, crossed the eight lanes of traffic and four of bicycles on the Bund and entered a pedestrian underpass.

And there he was. As always. The ancient man with his

arhu and begging bowl. Fong spread out a piece of newspaper and sat on the dirty tiles across from the old man. He pressed his cheek into the coolness of the tile wall.

"The weight is heavy on you tonight," the old man said.

"Yes," Fong agreed.

"Things must be permitted to end to allow other things to begin."

Fong nodded but said nothing.

"The weight of ghosts can crush a man."

To this Fong was afraid even to nod his head, "Play something for me, Grandpa – and help me forget." Fong slipped some yuan notes from his pocket and placed them in the begging bowl.

The man's ancient fingers touched the arhu's strings. The instrument's unearthly tones bounced like living things off the hard tile surfaces of the tunnel then fell from on high like diving birds into Fong's ears where they fell, fell, fell through endless space to the still terribly deep pond beneath that was him.

CHAPTER ELEVEN

The next morning when Fong opened his office door he saw a bearded white man behind his desk, sitting in his chair. With a kind of jolly hop, this fireplug of a man stood up and, with his right hand extended, approached Fong, "Your assistant let me in. In fact, he was in here when I arrived."

Fong was about to reply that he had no assistant then understood that Shrug and Knock must have been in his office. That one never learns! He turned his thoughts back to the Long Nose in front of him.

The man wore large glasses on his oval face, which Fong guessed were designed to keep his eyes apart, because whenever he laughed, which clearly happened often, his face threatened to fold in at the centre. He was barrel-chested and had tufts of greying hair sprouting from the top of his tight-fitting shirt. The man must have thought this stylish but no Chinese man would be caught dead wearing clothing that was too tight. And of course few had chest hair.

Something about the man made Fong want to laugh out loud. He didn't because he was too stunned by what Westerners call serendipity but what he knew was actually meaning manifesting itself. He'd seen this strange white man before! But where? The man was already talking, something about being the West's foremost Shakespearean scholar. Fong nodded. He wanted to speak to an expert on Shakespeare's plays in performance because he wanted to follow up Geoff's assertion that "great directors put their present lives into everything they direct," and Geoff was, as far as Fong was concerned, a great director. Fong suspected that clues to what was going on in Geoff's life were embedded in his production of *Hamlet*. To that end, they'd found this man for him to interrogate.

"Donny," the man said.

"That's your name?" Fong asked.

"Donny. Some call me Don."

"And you're a . . . "

"A professor of dramatic literature in performance."

Fong thought about that for a moment. Literature in performance, what could that mean? An image of books dancing about a stage spouting lines leapt into his head.

"Would you like to see my passport?"

"Sure," Fong said, while he thought, "Why is this man offering me his passport?"

Donny handed him his American passport and Fong quickly understood. There it was. Don or Donny had a Class 2 visa status. Only politicians and big businessmen came in on higher classification. Directors and actors came in usually as Class 4 or Class 5 visitors. It had always pissed off Fu Tsong that academics were allowed into China on a higher-status visa than artists who came over to actually do something. Fong handed back the passport, didn't know where to start, so he said, "So you teach."

"For almost thirty years."

Fong wanted to say those were probably the longest thirty years of most of his students lives but didn't. "Tell me your name again."

"Don. Donny to my friends."

Fong stared at this pumpkin of a man.

Donny put a thick, hairy fist on the desk and assumed a professorial air, clearly something he had done many times before. "At any rate, I saw Mr. Hyland's *Hamlet*. Very interesting."

"Good," Fong said nodding, not knowing whether it was his turn to speak or not.

"It was good, quite good, I thought," Don said answering a question that Fong had not asked.

"Me too, I thought it was excellent."

"Are you an aficionado, Detective?"

"No, but I liked Mr. Hyland's *Hamlet* very much."

"I see," Don or Donny said noncommittally.

"Was there anything about the production that struck you as out of the ordinary . . . ?"

"Donny. I prefer it to Don, which is so East Rutherford, don't you think?"

Fong had absolutely no idea if he thought that or not but said, "Donny. So was there anything that struck you as unusual in Mr. Hyland's production?"

"Well, the opening . . . "

"Yes, I grant that." Fong knew that the opening with Hamlet almost naked and screaming on the platform was unique, but he assumed that anything going on in the director's head would worm itself into the production on a more subliminal level. "Other things . . . "

"Call me Donny."

Donny! Donny, Donny, Donny! Got it! The memory came back whole. Donny! It was years ago and his wife Fu Tsong had dragged him to the theatre. Sometimes she made him accompany her on what she called her "obligation."

"Come on, Fong. Do it for me," she'd said as they rushed to flag down a cab on Nanjing Lu. Fong agreed, held out his badge and a cab immediately swerved across six lanes of traffic to pick them up.

He loved Peking Opera, but modern spoken drama left him cold.

"What is this play?" he asked as the cab busted its way through a twelve-cyclist-deep line.

"This new thing, Fong. About the Qin Dynasty."

"A new play about the Qin Dynasty? Does that make any sense?"

She gave him a be-good look.

Their seats were, thankfully, near the back of the auditorium. He was pleased to see that the four seats in front of them were empty. If boredom gave way to yet more boredom he could put up his feet and take a snooze.

She looked at him with an oddly sad expression on her face then put a slender index finger to her lips, "Shh." The buzzer sounded and the play began although that did nothing to silence the audience who continued to chat, prepare full dinners at their seats and call across the auditorium when the fancy took them. Fong had brought along a snack, a dumpling wrapped in rice then steamed in a large grape leave, but he decided against eating it just yet.

The opening scene had something to do with trouble in ol' Xian, a princess, a tax collector – something else. Fong had already lost interest and was about to "assume the position" when three white people and an elderly Chinese lady hustled in and took the seats in front of them.

The Chinese lady was clearly a party member with pretences of importance. Fong'd met her type before. She was of little interest to him, but the Caucasians were another matter. As head of Special Investigations in Shanghai he'd dealt with a lot of North Americans. But none quite like these three! Two were women. One was tall and darkish, pretty but somewhat put-upon – Tall Lady; the other, who Fong surmised was married to the man, was short and had a wide expanse of curly hair – Big Hair. Fong wondered for a moment if her head was just very wide. The man, Donny they called him, seemed to think he had to look after the women although it was obvious that these women needed no supervision.

The Chinese woman, one of the 40 million-odd Madame Cheungs in the People's Republic of China, spoke loudly although she seemed to have only a fleeting grasp of the English language. Even her Mandarin seemed a bit shaky. Fong wondered if some malicious bureaucrat had stuck these three white people with a person suffering from gentle dementia. It wouldn't be the first time it had happened.

Suddenly the play inexplicably stopped and a long pantomime followed wherein most of the costumes were paraded.

"Lots of hats," Fong whispered.

"Careful," Fu Tsong hissed back.

Then Tall Lady leaned over toward Big Hair and said, "They do talk in this play, don't they? I mean this isn't a mime, is it? I hate mime."

"Really?" asked Donny in mock surprise.

"I hate mime's nasty little cousins, ventriloquists, too," said Big Hair.

"Ventriloquists are only mimes with attitude," said Tall Lady.

"Mimes who can't keep their mouths shut," said Big Hair.

"Mimes whose lips move," chirped Donny.

Listening to the chatter of the three Caucasians was an unexpected treat. Fong wanted to applaud. Give a hardy "Hoa." Cleverness, never much in abundance in this kind of theatre, was a welcome relief.

Madame Cheung responded, "Is noble – no?"

Donny gave a get-this-broad look to Big Hair and Tall Lady then put an expansive smile on his face and turned to Madame

Cheung, "It's a fascinating mix of styles, the surreal and the naturalistic."

Tall Lady let out a groan.

Fu Tsong whispered in Fong's ear, "I like her and she has taste too." The warmth of her breath made his heart miss a beat.

The play finally got to its story line, something about an emperor whom everyone was trying to kill because he was sleeping with too many young girls in an effort to maintain his youth or something. Fong couldn't understand why the other characters didn't just rush at him and knock him off the stage and save everyone a lot of aggravation.

Near the end of the act, a large map lowered inexplicably from the flies.

Madame Cheung leaned over Donny and intoned, "It is a map."

Tall Lady asked, "How long has this play been running?" The question was relayed down the line to Madame Cheung and the answer was relayed back from Donny, who announced completely straightfaced, "Just over an hour and a half."

Tall Lady let out a loud, "Oh, god" and returned to some deep inner space.

In the middle of the fourth scene, someone offstage began singing "I Did It My Way" – very loudly. Fong saw the back muscles of Big Hair begin to quiver, then she spluttered. Madame Cheung leaned over and said gravely, "Flank Sinatra."

"Flank?" exploded Donny. That was too much for Tall Lady who burst out laughing. But Donny kept his face blank and asked smoothly, "Is that part of the play?"

Madame Cheung pondered Donny's question for a moment then the map came down again and she pointed out, "It is a map."

In the next scene, someone, Fong had by this time totally lost track of the characters, committed suicide. Fong cheered.

Many others in the audience joined him. Every bad actor killed is a step in the right direction. Upon the death, the curtain fell and the house lights came up. Before the Caucasians could rise, the intrepid Madame Cheung announced loudly, "Good. It's intercourse," and headed to the bathroom.

The three foreigners managed to hide their faces but Fu Tsong, who had been following the scene in the row ahead as closely as Fong, lost it completely. Donny pointed at Fu Tsong and then broke out laughing. Through his laughter he said to Big Hair, "I like her," to which Big Hair, tears of laughter streaming down her face, said, "I can see why." The Tall One had crumpled in her chair clutching her sides and barked out, "Good, it's intercourse. And she's an English teacher."

Donny announced to all and sundry, "I've been bored to tears in theatres in every language in every country in the world." To which the Tall One replied through tears of laughter, "And whose fault is that?"

Donny was still talking, evidently oblivious to that fact that Fong had just taken a rather extended internal voyage. "As I said, Detective, I've been bored to tears in theatres in every language in every country in the world."

"And whose fault is that?" Fong replied, immensely pleased with his own cleverness. Donny looked at him. "That sounds familiar."

"Really?"

"Yeah, but I can't quite place it," Donny said, for the first time eyeing Fong as something more than a student asking for an extension on a term paper.

Fong avoided Donny's eyes and said, " Let's start with the text of the play. It's usually cut, isn't it?"

"Yes. It's only a myth that *Hamlet*'s a quick play. It's ponderous and long, so everyone cuts it."

"Was Mr. Hyland's cutting unusual?"

"Well, he left in the Reynaldo scene and the whole Rosencrantz and Guildenstern plot, which is out of the ordinary. As well, he played up the relationship between Polonius and Claudius. Made Polonius a smart guy in disguise."

"Yes, he did," said Fong. "Is the Reynaldo scene about spying?"

"Yes. Reynaldo is sent to follow Laertes and make sure that he behaves himself and cover for him when he doesn't behave himself. Yes, Mr. Hyland also left in the Voltaman plot."

"More spying and deceiving?"

"Yes and of course so is the R and G plot."

"R and G?"

"Rosencrantz and Guildenstern – ah, gentle Rosencrantz and wise Guildenstern."

"These are the men sent to murder Hamlet on the boat to England."

"Yes, but Hamlet finds their orders, switches the names on the letter and the two of them are murdered."

"Spying again."

"That's a little crude, but yes spying, if you will. He's also used what's thought of as the American cutting. By removing the subplot of Fortinbras the entire evening drifts toward the demise of a great soul, Hamlet. It makes sense when you see the opening he's devised but it does make the evening more personal and less political. The Europeans have a tendency to make the play about succession and politics. For that you need the history of Fortinbras and he must arrive at the end to solve the problem." Donny smiled, "*Capiche?*"

"Pardon me?'

"You understand?"

Fong nodded. Oh, yes, he understood more than this odd bowling ball of a man could ever imagine. Geoffrey Hyland and spying. Geoffrey Hyland arriving without a visa three months ago. Geoffrey Hyland eluding his surveillance team for thirty-six hours. Geoffrey Hyland and two Beijing handlers. "Do you know much about Shakespeare's use of flowers, Donny?"

"Everything about Shakespeare's use of flora, I know."

"Everything?" Fong wanted to ask but let that slide. Instead he asked, "What did primroses mean in Shakespeare's writing?"

"They represented things unfinished. Things that die before they are old or done or consummated."

Fong thought about that then asked, "And marigolds?"

"Flowers for middle age – a mid-life flower." Donny smiled. His eyes twinkled. He was being impressive and he liked being impressive.

Fong nodded, "And forget-me-nots?"

A darkness crossed Donny's round features. A vein suddenly pulsed in his forehead just over his left eye. "Forget-me-nots? I don't believe there are any mentions of forget-me-nots in Shakespeare." The smile returned to his face. "But I'll check. That's what graduate students are for, don't you think?"

Fong had no idea if that was what graduate students were for but asked, "Anything else I should know about Mr. Hyland's *Hamlet* production?"

"Well there's the standard Laertes–Ophelia attachment."

"Attachment?"

"Well, Laertes does seem to be a little more than just expressing a brotherly concern for his sister."

"Thus his anger at Hamlet?"

"Absolutely. Well, there is also the fact that Hamlet killed his father and Ophelia committed suicide when Hamlet dumped her."

"Don't you think those two little things just might be enough to lead to a bit of animosity from Laertes toward Hamlet?"

"I guess it could, do that, that is," said Donny in all seriousness.

He guesses! Fong shook his head; he'd never understand academics. The watermelon of a man smiled. Fong didn't. "Thanks." He ushered Donny toward the door. The man was still talking. Then he stopped and looked at Fong for a long moment. "Hey, I've met you before."

"No, I'm sure you're . . . "

"No, I have a really good memory for faces. Yes. Fuck the Dean then do the Bishop!"

"Excuse me?"

"At that stupid play. Right. I saw you at that stupid play." Donny rubbed his hands in satisfaction then looked hard at Fong. "Hey, you were with a really pretty lady, right?"

"Right."

"An actress, right?"

"Right."

"Hey, how's she doin'?"

"She's dead. A long time ago."

"Sorry to hear that. Beautiful girl. Really beautiful."

Fong finally manoeuvred Donny out the door and shut it. He took a deep breath. That was hard. Too hard. Fu Tsong was still so completely present. So entirely there – her ghostly weight almost too heavy to bear – and Fong knew it.

Only the hulls of the junks that, before the war, used to ply the Su Zu Creek were still extant. In these rotting containers lived the poorest of the poor in Shanghai. The Su Zu Creek is not what is meant when real estate agents advertise "with river view." The stink of the creek announces its presence well before one sees the turgid, shallow waterway. But water is water and summer is summer so kids are in the creek – and so is the body of a woman who used to hand out keys at Geoffrey Hyland's guesthouse.

Two children throw a colourful button they pulled off one of their grandmother's blouses into the water then dive after it. It's a challenging game because the Su Zu Creek is thick with silt that is constantly churned up by wakes coming up the creek and produced by passing barges on the Huangpo River. It made every dive for the button an adventure. None more so than the dive when the young boy reached into the silt and touched something rubbery and yucky – something that had been a lady who gave out keys in Geoffrey Hyland's guest-house.

A pug-nosed Shanghai detective watched the flesh thing that used to be a body emerge from the creek's dark water. He'd been an investigating officer for almost thirty years and although he had only a few years left on the force, he wasn't looking forward to his retirement. With almost no money saved and very little pension, he knew his future was uncertain. After surviving all the regime changes in the Shanghai police force to be left maybe literally out in the cold struck him as particularly unfair but somehow infinitely Chinese. He smiled and indicated that the divers should put what was left of the body on the far shore. He didn't believe they'd find out much about the death of this old woman – or at least she seemed to be an old woman. The eels in the creek had already eaten away most of the extremities of the body, the gelatinous facial parts and the liver. He lit a cigarette and allowed himself a fulsome cough. Then he saw the button the boys had been diving for. It had snagged on a string extending from the pocket of her quilted Mao coat. He pulled on the string and out came a key. A key to what? There had been a tag attached to the key but the acidity of the creek had removed the writing. He bagged the key, checked for ID and, finding none, instructed the officers to remove the body. Old people died all the time. Some fell into the creek. Some were dropped there. He allowed the key to roll around in his palm and wondered how he'd find out into what lock this key fit.

The rest of Fong's afternoon was filled with disappointments – to be expected – but disappointments nonetheless. Like clock-work, cops appeared at his office door with confirmations of alibis from the theatre people. The only one of any real interest was the confirmation of Rosencrantz and Guildenstern's alibi. Several gay men, after a little bullying, verified Rosencrantz and Guildenstern's presence at the party. Not surprisingly, both party members who had been named by the actors had denied any knowledge of either the gathering or Rosencrantz and Guildenstern. Both had demanded Fong's phone number and made the usual threats. That was fine with Fong. He filed away the two men's names and phone numbers. They could prove to be very useful at some time in the future. Then he sat back in his office chair and stared at the Pudong out his window. The dozens of new buildings stood proud against the fading August sunlight. He thought about how the Pudong only ten years ago had been nothing but a swamp across the Huangpo River. Now it was the Pudong Industrial District, the very centrepiece of the new China. Fong thought about how power had brought those buildings into being. He thought about how power worked. Then he thought about how good it was to have diverse attitudes like those of the two gay party members within the halls of power of the Middle Kingdom and he allowed himself a smile.

It was the third locksmith that the Shanghai detective went to that informed him that the key was newly minted and proba-bly was from a guesthouse because it had markings that indi-cated there could be a master key to override it.

A guesthouse? This could be trouble. Guesthouses were used by foreigners. He was a basic Shanghai street cop. He did-n't deal with crimes that had to do with foreigners. That was done by those damn snobs down on the Bund. Well, so be it. He picked up the phone and gave Special Investigations a call.

The call was received at general dispatch at Special Investigations just before sunset. Because the general dispatcher was a party hack's son he didn't mark it as urgent. Since there was no way of knowing if it was a murder and no way of knowing if it was committed by a foreigner, he filed the gist of the report in the boxes for Fong, Li Chou and the commissioner and didn't give it a second thought. All three glanced at it before day's end. All three had more important things on their desks than the remains of an old lady who probably had too much to drink, hit her head on the side of the junk and fell into the creek.

In accordance with the department's new policy of limiting expenditures, an autopsy was put on hold. It wasn't until days later that Fong asked for the full report of the old lady's death that had the reference to a key to a guesthouse buried in the bottom.

CHAPTER TWELVE

BODIES AND ALIBIS

t was just past eight in the evening but the aggressive heat of the day still held a grip on the vast city. The morgue workers were packing up and heading home. Fong looked from Lily to the morgue slab where Geoff's body lay.

"I need you to sign off on the autopsy report as the head investigator, Fong," Lily said in her lilting Shanghanese.

Fong nodded but didn't take the pen Lily was holding out to him.

"So just do it. There's nothing more this corpse can tell us and our refrigeration allowance was halved in the last city budget. It won't be long before he begins to stink."

Fong couldn't take his eyes from the corpse. Over and over he punished himself with the thought: "Fu Tsong loved this man." He was shocked when Lily stood behind him and put her hands on his back – but he was glad for the contact. Lily moved in closer and whispered softly, "It's time this was returned to the earth."

Fong took one last look then nodded. "Thanks, Lily," he said in English.

"Nothing think of it, Short Stuff."

Fong took the pen from her, held the autopsy report close to his face then signed it.

"You need glasses," Lily said, taking back the document and her pen.

Fong was momentarily surprised that it was so obvious but he left that thought quickly as he realized that in the entire time he'd known Lily "You need glasses" was the only grammatically correct use of English he'd ever heard come out of her mouth. Maybe her English was improving and their daughter Xiao Ming stood a chance of speaking English properly.

"You're something, Lily," he said in English.

"Yeah. What but though is question," she replied.

"Nope," Fong thought. Linguistic improvement: strictly temporary.

Lily didn't like the look on her ex-husband's face so she shifted to Shanghanese, "So have you found out who this Long Nose was fucking just before he died?"

Once Fong was back on the street he called Chen. "Are our Beijing guests there?"

"Yes, and they're a bit annoyed, sir."

Fong smiled, "Good." He hung up and decided to walk back to the office. They'd made him wait at the prison, now they could cool their heels for a while in his office.

The heat had finally backed off a pace although it would most assuredly return with the dawn. The evening was just beginning to soften. As he walked Fong marvelled at the human reality that is Shanghai. His home. He passed by sidewalk barbers cutting hair for customers seated on small three-legged bamboo stools; and sidewalk bicycle repairmen, often referred to as maestros, who busied themselves stuffing fat red-rubber tubes back in tires; and sidewalk cobblers repairing shoes while surrounded by neat rows of upturned high heels from women's pumps; and sidewalk seamstresses working on foot-powered sewing machines. Shanghai lives on its sidewalks. You can buy anything there. Fong passed by sellers of sugar-covered fried dough and soda-fountain pop and ice-cream bars made from frozen soya, and repackaged Western candy bars, and pirated CDs and pirated audiotapes and pirated DVDs, and old couples sitting on ratty chairs, their pant legs rolled up to their thighs. The latest Hong Kong pop tune floats on the air. A five-spice egg-seller blocks one nostril with a filthy thumb and discharges the contents of the other nostril onto the cracked pavement just a quarter-inch to one side of her cook pot then looks up at Fong: "I missed," she cackles. A leather-skirted girl parades her legs as if she were the only person with gams in this part of the world. Passing by the Hilton, the quotient of expensive cars increases as do the number of pimps selling their wares. A shop window almost entirely covered with snakes coiling upwards, their blunt snouts pushing against the uppermost pane, draws Fong's eyes as do the large glass jars of dried country roots and herbs in the next store. A countrywoman carrying a filthy baby barely covered in rags approaches a man with a hand out and a plea for help. A pregnant woman crosses a busy eight-lane street with all the pride and confidence that only a woman carrying a child in a single-child society can have. The blunted trees in front of a walled former French estate release their scent to the night air adding a sweetness that was not there only moments before. Men hand out cheap flyers advertising dance clubs, inexpensive pants, Ye Sheng (literally wild food), appliance repairs, bundles of kindling and coal, bulk rice and of course young girls.

On a city wall, a black-and-white eight-photo object lesson shows a corrupt official being caught by the federal police, tried by a federal judge and hanged before the populace. The photo lab's work is better than in the famous fraudulent photo of Mao swimming the Yangtze, but the eight photos were frauds nonetheless – and everyone knows they are frauds.

Two elderly Go players attract a crowd crammed with Shanghai's most abundant commodity – unsolicited advice. A young street sweeper with a mask across her mouth moves her bound-twig broom slowly as she breathes in the street fumes that will first make her prematurely old, then collapse her lungs before she's forty. The sound of Western music draws Fong into Renmin Park where old couples practise the steps of Western ballroom dancing to the sounds from a CD player that gets its energy from a hand crank. Above the dancers, the Marlboro man leers down from his billboard, clearly suggesting that a smoke and a horse are all a real man ever needs. The park is filled – no seat is free. The heat backs off another pace allowing in the gentle breeze from the mighty Yangtze. A child in new clothes plays with a large plastic toy to the glee of his parents and all four grandparents. Fong wonders when the child will realize that the dreams of all six of these adults lies squarely on his slender shoulders. Just a different kind of ghostly weight.

In darkened doorways couples steal kisses, hands caress curves and clutch hardness only to be laughed at by the local crone. Nightclubs pour their relentless beat onto the streets and Mao-jacketed elders shake their heads in disgust. A young man holds onto a lamppost and vomits in the gutter as others watch but no one helps – the fear of disease from the West now alive on the streets of the great city.

A dark alley's mouth emits sounds of anger and a whimpered apology. Floral wreathes outside a storefront announce the opening of a new business and plead for good luck from whichever gods have not yet forsaken the secular state of the People's Republic of China.

The recyclers are out in force with their large metal tongs extracting scraps of paper from the sodden waste in the garbage cans. Then, as if on some unheard cue, jetting flares erupt from the seven tall chimneys down by the Huangpo River. Shortly thereafter clouds of dark smoke belch into the night sky – the city's garbage begins to incinerate.

And the people and the smells and the lives in motion – Shanghai. Home.

"Present your alibis, please," Fong said for the third time.

The two Beijing men didn't move. They certainly didn't answer Fong's request.

Fong got up from his desk and, turning his back on the Beijing men, stared out his floor-to-ceiling office window overlooking the Bund. Just getting these two into his office was a major coup – but it wasn't enough. At this point in a murder investigation gains were made by subtraction and he had to be sure he was right before he removed anyone from his list of suspects. So alibis had to be demanded and checked. Without turning back to the Beijing men, Fong said, "This is a murder investigation. The murder of a foreigner in Shanghai falls within my jurisdiction, not yours."

The younger Beijing man took a step to his left, putting himself right beside Fong in the window's reflection. "What did you find in Geoffrey Hyland's room?"

"Old books, stupid tapes and dirty underwear," Fong answered the reflection without turning back to the men. He was careful not to lie since these facts could be checked.

The older Beijing man took two oddly elegant steps making it a trio of reflections in the window. "You have been back to see Mr. Hyland's play, this *Hamlet*, twice since his death. Why?"

"To figure it out."

"What is there to figure out?"

"Mr. Hyland was a great artist. Great artists often include their present concerns in their art."

"So you wanted to see what 'concerns' of Mr. Hyland's life he put in the play?"

"Yes."

"So what was there?"

Fong hesitated for a moment. He could lie about this because the truths he found were ephemeral – not evidence but ethos.

"What did you find, Traitor Zhong?"

"Ghosts and ghosts of ghosts," Fong said. But even as he spoke he thought: "I have seen that damned play one too many times."

The older man examined Fong's face in the window's reflection. Finally he said, "Be careful, Traitor Zhong, be very careful."

Fong responded quickly, overriding the threat, "Was Mr. Hyland a spy?"

The younger man took a step toward Fong's back, but the older man shot him a hard look and he stopped. "Why do you want to know that, Traitor Zhong?" asked the older Beijing man calmly.

"Mr. Hyland's version of *Hamlet* strikes me as heavy on the spy stuff. Since you guys are the only ones I know who deal with spooks, I thought maybe there was a connection."

"I doubt that he was spying in any ordinary sense of the term," said the older man.

"And in an extraordinary sense of the term?"

The older man did that elegant moving thing again then said, "Perhaps."

"Ah," said Fong and turned to face the two Beijing men. "Now that we have that cleared up, where exactly were you two clowns on the night of Mr. Hyland's death, say between 11 a.m. and 6 a.m. the next morning?"

Eventually the Beijing men coughed up alibis. The younger one had been in a K-TV lounge until almost three and the older man had led a seminar on counterterrorism late into the night in one of Beijing's many Shanghai safe houses. Both were able to supply several names and addresses of people who could corroborate their stories.

Upon completing his answer and then threatening Fong in an entirely predictable fashion – Fong thought of it as just more blah-blah from Beijing – the younger Beijing man shouted a final warning and stormed out of Fong's office.

Fong stood and once more turned toward the window – this meeting was over.

Fong glanced up into the pane and was surprised to see the older Beijing man take a quick step toward him.

Fong turned.

Then the younger Beijing man reappeared in his office door. The older man stopped in his tracks, shouted a threat that Fong found oddly half-hearted then whirled on his heel and left the office followed closely by his younger partner.

Fong watched their retreating figures and wondered if he needed to recalibrate where he thought they – or at least the older Beijing man – might fit in all this mess.

And what a mess it was. Geoff's death was not a suicide, although he had no idea who murdered him or why.

Fong reminded himself that Geoff was smart. Geoff had tried to communicate with him through his business card – maybe he had tried to communicate in other ways. Geoff's *Hamlet* certainly was concerned with spying and his two Beijing keepers were clearly more interested in Geoff's comings and goings than in his death. "The play's the thing" Fong remembered from the front of Geoff's business card. It would be like Geoff to leave messages on both sides of the card.

He checked that his office door was locked, noted that Shrug and Knock was gone then headed toward the old theatre on the campus of the Shanghai Theatre Academy. Despite the fact that he had seen Geoff's *Hamlet* twice since the director's death, Fong had the gnawing feeling that he had overlooked something – something obvious.

CHAPTER THIRTEEN

A TRIP AND A CD-ROM

After two days and nights travelling on local trains and buses, Joan Shui was 20 miles south of Shanghai. That night, she slept in the back room of a peasant's hut on some dirty straw with the pigs and two other small furry animals she couldn't identify, although she was told they were harmless.

She had been passed smoothly from one Dalong Fada escort to the next and, although the officials' demand to produce her papers increased as she neared Shanghai, no one had asked her to open the smelly bundle she carried on her back. In fact, the stinkier she got, the less interested officials were in her.

A pig cuddled up to her back, oh well, a little more stink couldn't but help. Yes dear, in this profession body odour is your friend. As she drifted off, she could just make out the angry whispers of this last escort's wife, who evidently was not as loyal to the cause as her husband.

Joan awoke in the middle of the night. Without a watch she had no idea what time it was. A second pig had nestled into her back and was snoring loudly in her ear. She'd heard worse at the Calden Inn. But it wasn't the pig's snoring that had awakened her.

Just for a moment Joan Shui couldn't catch her breath, as if her lungs had, for an instant, forgotten how to work.

Fong sat at the back of the old theatre. The day's heat had been trapped in the ancient building. Now, at almost two in the morning, it was obvious that the heat would keep its hold on the building through the night. Fong rolled up the bottoms of his pant legs so they were over his knees. Not a lot of relief, but some. He forced himself to think through the last time he had seen Geoff alive. It began with the Canadian director coming onstage while Fong was at the back of the auditorium. It ended with Geoff slipping Fong his business card, on the back of which were penned the words: *Help me, Fong.*

Fong sat in the same seat now that he had sat in then and slowly rewound his mental tape, making himself put the events in sequence. Geoff had said, "Fuck me with a stick, what brings your sorry ass here?" Fong had noted at the time how odd the words were, coming from Geoff's mouth. Then Geoff had called for a run of the play from the top. He'd hopped off the stage and headed toward Fong. He was followed by his translator Da Wei at a respectful distance and then by the two Beijing keepers and the two Screaming me-me's.

Fong stopped – well no, not stopped, startled into a new kind of waking. Was that the first time Geoff had known he was sitting there at the back of the theatre? If Geoff were trying to communicate with him, which was evident from the plea for help on the back of his business card, then he may have been sending messages from the very first time he knew Fong was watching. It had never occurred to Fong before but perhaps Geoff knew he was in the theatre from the very moment, the instant, that he'd arrived. It had been that way in the past. Geoff had that kind of intuitive knowledge of the spaces in which he worked.

Fong remembered a moment right after he arrived when Geoff seemed literally to stop in mid-air. Was that Geoff's response to knowing he was sitting at the back of the theatre? Maybe. If that were true, then Geoff's "Fuck me with a stick" may have been said to bring the two Beijing keepers into the open. To show them to Fong so that he would watch his mouth. That made some sense. Fong went back to his mental tape this time looking to see if there was other communication intended for him before Geoff claimed to discover him sitting in the back of the auditorium. Before "Fuck me with a stick," Geoff had talked to a few actors, set the fight director to work on the fight between Hamlet and Laertes and . . .

Fong felt a slither of cold make its way down his spine. Despite the heat he shivered. Geoff had spent all that time with the unusually large leather pouch used by Rosencrantz and Guildenstern to transport the letter instructing the ship captain to murder Hamlet. Geoff hardly ever bothered with props. In fact, Fong had never seen Geoff so much as touch a prop onstage, let alone be so concerned about something as inconsequential as a pouch. And he had done it onstage. Not in the wings with a props man but onstage – so Fong could see.

Fong rose and walked slowly toward the stage. A single bare light bulb hung from the ceiling upstage of the proscenium arch. It, too, seemed to sway with the turning of the earth – as Geoff had in the end.

Fong hopped up on the stage, turned and looked out at the darkness of the auditorium – a cavern drawing him, an emptiness needing filling. No, demanding filling. He had an impulse to speak, to open his heart, to unburden himself into the maw of the theatre – but he didn't. He knew he hadn't earned that right.

He crossed upstage of the proscenium arch stage right and flicked on the work lights. Harsh incandescence filled the cluttered space. Behind him Fong saw the props cage. He looked at the cheap lock. It took him a few minutes and a deep splinter to his left index finger, to force the hinges to pop.

Fong opened the door and stepped in. All the show's props, except the swords, were laid out on a large table with chalk marks around each and the name of each prop charactered beneath it. Fong admired the system – an oasis of organization in the chaos of the theatre. You look at the table, if any outline is empty, the prop is missing. Simple. Logical. Inexpensive. Very Chinese.

Fong reached over and picked up the satchel that had so concerned Geoff.

It was nothing very special, just a treated leather pouch sewn together with rough strips of hide. The front and back were lacquered stiff. He put a hand inside. Nothing. He turned it over and shook it. Nothing. He went to put it back on the table. As he did, the thing tilted and caught the light at an oblique angle. There. The slightest circular ridge on the outside of the leather. He picked up the pouch and tried to turn it inside out. It wouldn't turn. The lacquered stiffness prevented the piece from reversing. He examined the outside closely, nothing. He slid his hand into the pouch again slowly running his fingers around the rim then down the sides.

Halfway down, he felt an almost flat patch of something that could be glue.

Fong had had enough of being careful. He took out his pocketknife, slit the pouch along its seams and folded it back. The ridge was of glue as he had thought. And it sealed shut a slit in the leather.

Fong carefully broke the glue seal and opened the slit with his knife. Parting the lips of leather, he inserted his fingers.

Something hard.

A disk.

A CD-ROM.

By four in the morning Chen had the disk working in Fong's office computer. "Do you want me to open it?"

"Don't you want to know where it came from, Captain Chen?"

"I do want to know." That hung in the air for a moment like something heavy.

"Then ask, Captain Chen."

"I shouldn't have to ask. I'm part of this investigation or I'm not. If I'm part of this investigation then you should tell me without me having to ask."

"True, but perhaps it's safer that you don't know."

"Like you having a key to the theatre was safer for me not to know?"

This was the longest exchange he'd ever had with Chen without the country cop addressing him as "sir." "No, not like that, Captain Chen. Having a key to the theatre could, and I emphasize *could*, make me a suspect in a murder with which I had nothing to do. But what is on this CD-ROM could make you and I actually guilty of a crime."

"Unless we reveal the contents of the CD-ROM to the proper authorities."

No "sir" again but Chen didn't leave the office and go report to those proper authorities either. "What's the worst that could happen?"

Fong took a deep breath, "Ti Lan Chou Prison is not a happy place to spend the rest of your life."

Chen still didn't head toward the door, so Fong sat at the computer and said, "Show me how to start this thing, Captain Chen."

"The CD-ROM, sir?"

"Yes, Chen," Fong said, "the CD-ROM."

Chen opened the CD-ROM drive then stood back to allow Fong some privacy as he interfaced with a ghost who performed in response to the click of a mouse.

"Hello, Fong." Geoff's voice was ever so slightly out of sync with his lips. "I could use that old saw of 'If you're watching me now, then you've followed my clues.' To be frank, I knew you would.

"I used to hate you, Fong. All I wanted after Fu Tsong's murder, and yes I still believe you murdered Fu Tsong, was to punish you. It helped me, that anger, for a while. It gave me a purpose, a goal to my days now that Fu Tsong was gone. Something else to love. Yes, I loved the idea of hurting you, Zhong Fong.

"But it fades. Unlike love – the desire for revenge fades. And when it did, a purposelessness set in. Monday became indistinguishable from Thursday, November from February, nothing took on any uniqueness. Everything felt and was the same as everything else. Nothing became important or silly or insightful or stupid or lyric or banal or . . . well, you understand me, don't you, Fong?"

That last was in a different tone than what had come before.

"Sameness stretched out all around me like a vast featureless white room. You know the first thing I discovered while I was lost in that big white room? Guess, Fong."

Geoff's image stayed on the screen as he sang a silly ditty and moved his head back and forth in time to the melody like a metronome. Suddenly he stopped singing and his head stopped moving.

"Time's up, Fong. Your answer please."

Geoff turned so he was in full profile and cupped his ear as if waiting for a far-off response.

"No answer, Fong? Fine. It's your choice. The answer is: all human beings are better for the very fact of loving. Loving anything. It almost doesn't matter what. And for most people that loving shows you the way out of the big white room. But I had nothing to love so I stumbled about for months until I chanced upon a door that led to yet another, and infinitely larger, white room in which I stayed for almost a year. Do you know what finally showed me the way out? Three, two, one – time's up.

Purpose. If you can't have love, you can at least have purpose! Finding a purpose showed me the way out of that fucking room. Humans need to have purpose. Seen the books in my room, Fong? Like the way I organized them for you? I did that just in case you missed my clues leading you to this little performance. Scientists call it a backup. I thought of it as another way to score a goal. It's a hockey image – sorry, Fong, I assume hockey isn't your game. Too bad. Great game, hockey. Really great." This last was said with genuine feeling. Surprising feeling.

"So . . . " Geoff took a long breath and shook his shoulders as if they had suddenly become tight with tension. Fong noticed that sweat was appearing on his upper lip.

Geoff smiled. "It just occurred to me that if you are watching this performance, I may be dead. Now there's an odd thought, don't you think? Be that as it may, after you stole Fu Tsong, saving Xi Luan Tu became my purpose."

Fong couldn't believe it. Xi Luan Tu, the Dalong Fada activist and China's most wanted man was Geoffrey Hyland's purpose! No wonder the two Beijing guys were interested in Geoff's comings and goings.

Chen cleared his throat.

Fong had forgotten the younger man was there. Fong clicked the Stop icon. "Leave now, Chen, and all you've heard is gobbledygook from a crazy Long Nose. Stay and you've crossed the line into something that Beijing no doubt will see as treasonous if we don't report it."

Chen didn't answer.

"Are you sure, Captain Chen?"

Chen didn't move.

Fong nodded and clicked the Play icon:"What follows, Fong, are the codes I was to use and a list of people willing to help get Xi Luan Tu to the safety of the West." Fong scrolled through the list of contact names and numbers quickly. "Xi

Luan Tu's fate is now in your hands – well, your eyes actually. And so are the fates of all those people on the list. I'm sure that the people who entrusted me with helping get Xi Luan Tu out of the Middle Kingdom would not approve of me giving you this information. But they do not know you like I do. Through Fu Tsong, you and I are a kind of lovers. Aren't we, Fong? Odd idea, isn't it? Come to think of it, what is the name of the relationship between husband and lover anyways?"

The word *rivals* bloomed in Fong's mind.

"At any rate, through Fu Tsong I know that you could not be a bad man. There was something quintessentially good about her. She could never love a bad man." Geoff took an odd pause then continued. "So back to spy stuff. Here's what you need to know, Fong. I've already managed to hide the cell phone with wireless Internet access that I was supposed to get to him. I taped it behind the toilet in the men's room at the theatre – in the second stall. I had twenty-five-thousand American dollars and several sets of ID – party card memberships, residency papers, job assignments, three or four other such items and passports – to give to Xi Luan Tu as well. But I had to burn those. I couldn't shake the two Beijing guys. Do you know how bulky twenty-five thousand US dollars are? I did manage to dump my two watchers for a day and a half but I couldn't make contact with Xi Luan Tu. The money and papers went up in flames just before I 're-emerged' into the company of my two Beijing keepers." Geoff smiled sadly then he seemed to brighten. "Seen *The Godfather*, Fong? That's how I got the idea where to hide the cell phone. Retrieve it, Fong. Make contact with someone on that list then get that phone to them. That's my part in this enterprise – my purpose if you will. My role in the drama that I wasn't able to complete because of the all-too-present presence of the two gentlemen from Beijing. So that's where the gun – I mean the cell phone is. Get it and get it to one of those contacts. They'll get it to Xi Luan Tu and he'll use it to contact another Dalong Fada operative who should have backup money and papers to get him safely to the West. That's all there is to it. Easy for a tough guy cop like you, Fong."

It looked as though Geoff wanted to say something more then decided against it. His image froze for an instant then disintegrated into pixels then the nothingness of digital nowhereness.

There were a few beats of profound silence in the room. Finally Chen spoke, "Shall I retrieve the phone, sir?"

Fong looked at this odd country cop with the potato-like facial features. "Do you understand . . . "

" . . . what I'm doing? Yes. Shall I retrieve the cell phone?"

"No, Captain Chen. I'll do that. I want you to figure out how to put a bug into it. I'll make that contact and deliver the phone but I want to be able to follow wherever that thing goes."

"Why?"

No "sir" again. "Because what Mr. Hyland was doing might have something to do with who murdered him. This is not a political case to me. This is a murder investigation, Captain Chen."

Chen nodded but didn't move.

"What, Chen?"

"We don't carry that kind of electronic equipment in our section of the department. We'll need to requisition it from central stores. Other people will know we're up to something." Then, to Fong's surprise, Chen smiled.

"Chen?"

"This could be one of those situations that could prove to be a problem or an opportunity, couldn't it, sir?"

Fong smiled then nodded in agreement.

Fong felt the icky warm wetness soak through the knees of his pants as he knelt facing the filthy toilet of the second stall in the men's room at the old theatre. He held his breath as he reached behind the toilet tank and, with the tips of his fingers, located the cell phone taped there. "Why do Long Noses take ideas from movies!" he hissed and let out the rest of the air in his lungs. He took in a short sharp breath. He'd smelled worse but at the moment he couldn't recall where. With his cheek pressed hard against the underside of the toilet seat he finally managed to get his left hand far enough behind the toilet tank and, with one mighty yank, ripped the cell phone free of its bonds.

Geoff had used some kind of wide grey sticky tape to adhere the phone to the tank. Fong looked at the tape. He'd never seen anything like it. He unstuck it from itself and marvelled at it. It would have so many uses! But then it must be so expensive, so wasteful, so Western.

As he left the stall he slid the cell phone with the wireless Internet connection into his pant pocket and wondered what to do with the tape. Then he wondered about Westerners and their love of movies. He remembered an old joke during the Vietnam-war era. It seemed that an American president, Johnson he believed, announced at a public gathering that he had seen a movie called *Patton* and it had inspired him to invade Cambodia. The joke was: here was the first time in history that a war was based on a movie not a movie based on a war.

Joan's arrival in Shanghai was somewhat less high profile than the first time she had come to the great city. Then she'd landed at Hong Qiao International Airport only to be detained by an overzealous immigration officer. She'd been saved from that indignity by the arrival of Wu Fan-zi who, for ten days and nights, became her reason to live. This time, with what appeared to be just a filthy bundle on her back, she trudged the last 9 miles along the side of a busy highway in the morning darkness surrounded by thousands of peasants. Hidden in her filthy bundle was US$25,000 and four sets of fake ID and passports – part of what was needed to get Xi Luan Tu out of Shanghai and to the West.

Back in his office with the cell phone safely in his pocket, Fong activated Geoff's CD-ROM. He fast-forwarded through the lists and copied the names, numbers and code words with their meanings onto a pad. Then he hit the Eject button and removed the CD-ROM from the computer.

A milky morning light was just peeping over the horizon. Another day of heat clearly lay ahead. He called in Chen.

"Sir?"

"When I played this CD-ROM, did the computer copy it?"

"Copy it, sir? Oh, you mean back it up."

"I guess. Did it?"

Chen sat at the machine. Two clicks and a scroll down later and he gave Fong the bad news. "The machine is set up with an auto backup. And it takes cookies as well. Not all the digital material may have been burnt onto the hard drive but some of it probably was."

"Burnt means copied, right?"

"Right."

"And cookies?"

"Cues to the computer as to how to find material that is stored on the drive. The term is American and I'm told refers to pieces of pastry left behind so children can find their way out of the woods."

Fong nodded. For a moment he wondered why the children would use cookies to mark their path out of the woods. Wouldn't animals eat the cookies? Then he wondered why he was wondering about stuff like this. He looked at Chen. The man was waiting for instructions. Okay. But destroying evidence was even more of a crime than having evidence and not reporting it. Fong would save Chen the problem if he knew how to destroy the CD-ROM and the hard drive – but he didn't know how to safely get rid of either.

"Do you want the copy erased, sir?"

"Is that possible?"

Chen's face took on a funny look. Fong had no idea what that look might mean.

"Well, Captain Chen?"

"You want to be certain there is no copy on the hard drive, right, sir?"

"Yes, Chen. That's what I want."

Chen reached into his pant pocket and took out a penknife. He tilted the computer to expose the screws in the back. "You understand what this means, Captain Chen?"

"Yes. Yes, I do." He undid the screws with a remarkable dexterity. Then, removing the case he snapped out the hard drive.

"That's the hard drive, right?"

"Yes it is," he said holding it out to show Fong. "Now give me the original CD-ROM." Fong hesitated. "You want there to be no trace of this, don't you, sir?"

Fong nodded.

"Then I need to destroy the CD-ROM along with the hard drive." Chen's hand was still extended toward Fong.

Fong wanted to protect Chen from committing the offence of destroying evidence but he didn't know how. Then it occurred to Fong that once he gave over the CD-ROM and the hard drive Chen would have all the evidence he'd need to really hurt him.

Fong trusted Chen. But now it was not just his future he was handing over to this ugly country police captain whom he had first met on far-off Lake Ching, on the lake boat with the seventeen dead foreigners, and who now lived with his ex-wife Lily – it was the lives of all the people implicated by the material on that disk.

Could Captain Chen be trusted with those lives?

Maybe Captain Chen thought that Dalong Fada was a dangerous enemy that needed to be stomped out. Maybe he feared cults in general. Maybe there was a secret Captain Chen that

Fong had never met who harboured ambitions within the Shanghai police force and would use information like this to advance his own career.

Maybe Chen was as irrationally jealous of him as he had been of Geoff.

Fong stared at the man. "How's my daughter, Xiao Ming?"

Chen blushed, "Getting used to having me around. She knows I'm not you. It's clear she misses you. But I try to give her what little I can. I am not much of replacement for you, sir."

Chen's answer was so devoid of guile that Fong relaxed. Chen was exactly what he seemed to be – an honest, absolutely good man. And loyal. Xiao Ming was lucky to have such a man in her life.

All that was true, but what Fong failed to consider was: loyal to whom?

Fong handed Chen the CD-ROM. Chen then wrapped the CD-ROM with the hard drive in newsprint he took off Fong's desk, turned on his heel and headed toward the door.

"How're you going to destroy those things?"

"I'm not. There's no sure way to do that. I'm going to lose them."

"What?"

"I'm going to take a stroll across the new bridge to the Pudong and they're going to happen to fall into the muddy waters of the Huangpo River. The silt is so thick there that even if they sent divers down there's no chance they'd ever find them."

He smiled. Fong smiled back.

"That's all right, sir?"

"It's fine . . . and thanks."

As the door closed behind Captain Chen, Fong wondered at the new alliances that were now central to his life. Fu Tsong used to quote Shakespeare about just this sort of thing. Something about circumstance making strange bedfellows. Then Fong stopped. Another of Fu Tsong's favourite quotations from English writing had popped unbidden into his consciousness: "What a tangled web we weave when first we practise to deceive."

Fong eyed the first number on the list he had taken from the CD-ROM. He knew there was no point trying to find an address from the phone number because Shanghanese used cell phones almost exclusively and almost everyone prepaid for time used so there was no billing required. In theory, cell phone buyers had to give an address when they got a phone number, but everyone lied. Even Fong, on a reflex, had lied when he got his first cell phone. In fact, there was no incentive to tell the truth since there was not even a remote chance of being caught for such a violation of the law. Shanghanese purchase thousands of cell phones a week. In fact, without cellular technology there was no way that the economic miracle that had taken place in Shanghai could have happened. It would have been an insurmountable expense to have wired all of Shanghai.

Fong punched in the number. The cell phone was answered on the third ring, "*Dui.*"

The accent was Shanghanese, the background noise that of a large kitchen.

Fong spoke using the first word in the coded sequence. There was a brief silence on the other end. Then a coded word was buried in the man's response. Fong looked at his notes to find the word's meaning. The word was soup – *tang* – and it meant be careful, I'm being watched.

The man on the other end of Fong's call was not the only man being watched at that time. Captain Chen's stroll along the bridge to the Pudong was observed as was his entrance to central stores and his exit with a small plastic-covered package – by another set of wary, feral eyes. These eyes belonged to Shrug and Knock, who quickly reported to Li Chou.

As Chen returned to Fong's office with the bug for the cell phone that had the wireless Internet access for Xi Luan Tu, the desk phone in Fong's office rang. "It's for you, Captain Chen," Fong said holding out the receiver.

Chen hesitantly took the phone, listened for a moment then said, "Thanks. I owe you one or maybe two." He handed the phone back to Fong.

"Captain Chen?"

"It's good to have friends in low places, sir. They help situations become opportunities not problems."

Fong laughed. It was the first joke that Chen made that Fong understood. Chen blushed. "Is your friend more powerful than our friend's friend, Captain Chen?"

"Much, because he's lower."

"And you're sure that you were followed?"

"Oh, yes, quite sure. They didn't pay any attention to what I dropped off the bridge to the Pudong but I made sure they saw me pick up these. " Chen smiled and unwrapped the two electronic bugs. One was attached to the other. Then he held out his hand for the cell phone with Internet access.

As Fong gave him the phone, a darkness crossed Captain Chen's features. "What?"

"Remind me how following the cell phone will help us find who killed Mr. Hyland?"

"Mr. Hyland was involved in a pretty risky enterprise. Perhaps someone in Dalong Fada, perhaps someone in the Beijing security services, perhaps someone who's only peripherally involved with all this had it in for Mr. Hyland. I don't know exactly, Captain Chen, but at this point in a murder investigation every lead has to be tracked down."

Chen thought about that for a moment then asked, "Are you going to tell the commissioner about the data on the CD-ROM?"

Fong hesitated then said, "No."

"I assume you haven't told the two men from Beijing who were with Mr. Hyland either?"

Fong said nothing.

"I see," said Chen. He opened the cell phone and planted one of the electronic bugs. "This tiny guy sends out a signal that I can receive on my PalmPilot. It lets you and me track the phone wherever it goes. And this little fellow . . . " he said, placing the second bug in the cell phone snuggly against the first one, ". . . this one lets them follow the phone too – as long as we want."

"And when we don't want them to follow it anymore?"

"I dial 555 555 555 1."

"And dialling that number . . . ?"

"Cancels the signal from their bug and starts up a new signal from our third little friend." Like a magician at a country fair, Chen produced a third bug from the recesses of one of his baggy pant pockets and held it in the palm of his hand.

Fong watched Captain Chen complete his task.

He did not fail to notice that all of Chen's last statements were said without the use of the word: sir.

CHAPTER FOURTEEN

THE HIDING MAN

Xi Luan Tu hoped it was like being a mist inside a fog – either that or this hiding in plain sight was just a way of fooling himself. No doubt the truth would be evident soon enough. He glanced over his shoulder. The southern alley entrance to what as a kid he called "the warrens" was just a quick bolt away. As boys, he and his brother had explored this massive underground network of tunnels and caves that stretched for miles beneath the streets of Shanghai. Almost every section of the Old City could be accessed by one of the hundreds of underground alleyways. Some of them were now being widened for use in Shanghai's new subway system, but most of the passageways were still secret. The warrens ran beside, beneath and behind the buildings of the Old City. They had been used by thousands of Chinese people since their inception in the mid-1800s when the British, French and Americans had been given the only useful lands in Shanghai in the disgraceful *Treaty of Nanjing*. The Chinese had been forced from their homes and moved into the lowlands, the swamps by the river. At first, the warrens were a way for the Chinese to avoid the British and French rulers of their city. Year by year, Chinese hand by Chinese hand, they had expanded until they became an intricate underground world. A secret world. A world where white men were not welcome. Where a Chinese man could hide from the authorities. Tunnels, caves, stores of food and water, booby traps, false exits, culs-de-sac and abandoned subterranean pathways stretched, unmapped, for miles. Xi Luan Tu had grown up playing in the warrens. If things got too hot for him above-ground, he'd head for the warrens. It was his best chance – not to escape, because there were no escape routes out of Shanghai from the warrens, but to hide.

"How much?" the gruff man in front of his stand demanded as he pointed at the undulating carpet of life formed by the thousands of grub pupae that seethed in the barrel. Xi Luan Tu quoted him a reasonable price but not too low. He didn't want his fellow market pupae-sellers to take too much note of the "new guy." His forged vendor's licence had been arranged by a follower whose father used to occupy the spot. If asked, Xi Luan Tu would inform a questioner that he was the nephew of the man who used to sell here and that he had recently arrived from Sichuan Province.

"Too much," said the potential customer and moved on down the alley to the next grub pupae-seller.

The live things – he thought of them as grubs-in-training – continued their blind movements in the barrel. For three days he'd hidden in that very barrel while federal officers mounted sweeps in an effort to find him. Without the Dalong Fada exercises he would never have managed to maintain his sanity. The moment he lost the sense of himself as merely part of a much greater whole – the moment that he believed that he was the whole in and of himself – then the pain, the fear and misery took hold of him and led him toward madness.

He put his hands into the barrel of moving grub pupae and allowed their motion to become part of his existence. "Like spreading the molecules of yourself wide," he thought, "and allowing all that space in."

It was precisely as he completed that thought that two federal officers rounded the corner and headed right toward him.

Xi Luan Tu took another quick glance over his shoulder – he could beat them to the warrens' entrance if he had to – and once there, he could lose them.

At the same time on the far side of the great city, Joan Shui was holding on to a lamppost and trying to stop the world from spinning. Wu Fan-zi seemed to be everywhere in the city. It was as if he'd just left a room whenever Joan entered or ducked into a doorway, as she approached or turned the far corner, as she turned onto a street. She'd been with her "fireman" almost every moment of her first trip to Shanghai. Now she was here, shorn hair and all, and he was not.

She found herself drawn to the Hua Shan Hospital where she had seen him last. Where the bomb set by the American who called himself Angel Michael had ended Wu Fan-zi's life. It was in there their hearts had met. It was in there they had seen each other. It was in there she lost him forever.

"Move along."

Joan looked at the young man in the ill-fitting brown uniform with the insignia on his shoulder. Who was he talking to in that tone of voice?

"Move along, you!"

"Was he talking to me?" Joan thought. "I'm no stupid peasant who . . ." then she stopped even the process of that thought. It was good that he thought her nothing more than some stupid countrywoman who had come into Shanghai to beg on the streets. As long as people like him thought that way, she was safe.

"Move your fat ass!" he screamed at her.

Now that's a bit much. Peasant yes, stupid maybe, fat ass never. But she bobbed her head and did a bit of waving with her dirty hands, as if she couldn't understand his city accent then she put down her head and moved along.

She needed to find a phone kiosk.

She turned a corner and entered a crowded street market that ran down both sides of a narrow alley. The smell of rotting fish assailed her nose and swarms of fat flies circled her head then landed on, and seemed to taste, her filthy skin. She swatted them away only to be assaulted by the fish stink again. The gutted fish on the monger's dirty wooden table weren't even on ice. Those yet to be gutted swam in the brownish water of a rubber tub. A man wearing a nicely tailored suit approached the table and pointed at a large carp in the tub. The fishmonger reached into the brackish water and grabbed the fish by the tail. The thing thrashed in an effort to free itself from the monger's grip but the merchant wasn't about to let it go until the buyer gave his okay. They bartered briefly as the fish arched its body in protest. A price was settled on. The fishmonger stunned the thing with a smack of a short two-by-four then gutted it and wrapped it in old newsprint, using his right hand to get his money and his left to shove the guts beneath his table. The pile of guts was the source of the stink that attracted the flies. The gap-toothed fishmonger finished thanking the man in the good suit then screeched at Joan, "This not for you. This real fish. This for real people." Then he made a gesture with his hands toward her, not unlike what he should have done to the flies that encircled his table. Joan resisted the impulse to tell this merchant exactly where he could put his comments and forced her way through the crowded market.

Shanghai was even more densely populated than Hong Kong. She didn't think that possible, but it was. She finally found a phone kiosk and got in line. She needed to call the number she'd memorized from the e-mail. A half-hour and several nasty comments later, she finally got up to the kiosk, paid the two yuan and placed her call. An answering machine picked up and quickly gave an address then added, "Programmed cell phone there under curb. Pick it up and hit number three once." Then the answering machine cut off.

Moving to Xinzha Lu, Joan found a bus shelter with a Shanghai street map and oriented herself. It took her two hot hours of walking to get to the address she'd gotten from the answering machine. She passed by the address twice before it was clear enough of people for her to lean down as if adjusting the bundle on her back, reach beneath the cement overhang above the sewer grate and extract the small cell phone that had been put there for her between two bricks. Once she had the phone, she faced another problem. Looking the way she did, it would be incongruous that she owned a cell phone. So she had to find a place to use the phone where no one could see her. Not an easy thing to do amidst Shanghai's 18 million souls.

And prying eyes in this city could also report. She remembered the eyes of the man across from her in the fourth-class hard-seat train car. The way they bore into her and seemed to glory in the prospect of reporting her. "We Chinese enjoy the failings of our compatriots too much," she thought, "and although this may be part of the Chinese character, it had grown exponentially under Communist rule." More reason to promote an opposition like Dalong Fada.

She meandered, drawn by some force beyond her comprehension, to the Old City. Once there, the pace slowed. The dankness took over. There was little or no commerce here. Just lives lived in the shadow of the great. And alleyways. Dark alleyways that at this moment in Joan's life were her friends.

She reviewed the codes in her head before she hit the number three on the phone. The welcome code was given in response. Then she identified herself. It took a moment for the man on the other end to speak. Then he whistled into the phone and said, "They're bringing in the heavy artillery, are they?"

"I guess."

"Do you know the Temple of the City God?"

"No, but I can find it."

"Good. Go in the front entrance and buy seven sticks of

incense. Kneel and hold them between your palms as if you're ready to light them. I'll find you."

"How long will I have to do that?"

"As long as it takes."

"But won't it look suspicious if I hold the sticks and don't light them?"

"Hold them for a while, then as if you haven't decided on your prayer, put them back in your pocket and walk the grounds. It will not appear odd. Just another Chinese person anxious not to waste the cost of seven incense sticks on a frivolous request of the gods. Then come back as if you've made up your mind what you want to pray for and if I'm not there yet, go through the process again."

"Until you find me?"

"Yes. Until I find you."

Oddly enough, Joan didn't feel funny holding the seven incense sticks. She had had a moment of dread when she realized that the little money she had been given might not be enough to buy seven sticks of incense. The irony of it almost made her do a very unpeasant-like thing – laugh out loud. Here she had US$25,000 in her bundle and yet it was possible she didn't have enough money to buy seven stupid incense sticks. However, when she upended the cheap plastic change purse her contact on the ferry had supplied her, she found just enough.

With the sticks in hand, she opened one of the large wooden doors of the first pavilion. Before her was a pleasing room with hand-carved mahogany rails and three black lacquered screens. The floor was a much-worn marble. She walked through the quiet room and down a set of dark hardwood steps to the prayer chamber with its towering statues and kneeling pads. She waited for a moment then knelt. To her surprise, time seemed to slow down and sounds faded into the distance. She felt at ease.

She had never celebrated the passing of her lover Wu Fan-zi. And now, with the incense sticks in her hand, she had the opportunity.

She rubbed the sticks between her palms and in her heart sang his name.

Forty minutes later, a man knelt beside her with seven incense sticks in his hands. He touched his head to the ground then righted himself and rolled the sticks between his palms. As he closed his eyes he said, "The incense here is quite expensive, isn't it?"

She began to rock on her knees. "Yes, it is."

"Go up the stairs, out the back of the pavilion and look at the statue there. I'll walk past you. Follow me."

Chen came out of Fong's office so fast that he didn't even see Shrug and Knock until the poor man was prone on the ground. Chen immediately reached down to help him to his feet, "I'm terribly sorry. I hope your suit wasn't ruined. If it needs cleaning I will supply whatever money is necessary . . . "

"Get your stupid peasant hands off me! This jacket is new. It's my favourite." Shrug and Knock howled.

"I'm terribly sorry," Chen said as he pulled the jacket off of Shrug and Knock then shoved his hands into the inside pocket while he continued to shake dirt off the jacket, both inside and out.

"Enough, you . . . " Then Shrug and Knock let fly with a particularly demeaning comparison between Chen's facial features and lower parts of other human beings' anatomies, grabbed back his coat and walked back to his desk.

An hour later, Joan Shui was sitting across a table from her contact, who was clearly honoured to have her in his house. She thanked him for his help. She desperately wanted to ask to use his shower but she didn't. Cleanliness could be dangerous. Her disguise of filth had protected her so far and she wasn't going to change it now.

"Where is Xi Luan Tu?"

The man looked away.

"What?"

He took a deep breath then said, "He was supposed to contact us last week. All we know is that he is in Shanghai and he'll contact us through the Internet."

Joan's heart fell.

Finally on the fourth call to the sixth name on Geoff's list of numbers, Fong made contact – he thought of it as "getting through." Through what he wasn't quite sure.

"Are you the second wave?" the lightly lisped high Shanghanese female voice asked.

Fong flipped through the notes he'd made from Geoff's CD-ROM to get the code sequence right. "Yes, I am here to drive away the storm."

"Very clever," the voice said.

Fong noted the word *clever* as a "go ahead, all is safe" code word and said, "We should meet."

"We, no doubt, should." A moment passed then she spoke. When she did, her voice was harder than before, "The Catholic cathedral on Caoxi Beilu, just after evening prayers."

Fong didn't know what time that would be but he could find out on his own. "How will I recognize you?"

"You won't. I'll recognize you."

The phone went dead. For a moment Fong was at a loss: how could she recognize him? Then he got it – fuck! She thought he was Geoffrey Hyland, a white theatre director from Canada. He immediately punched redial on his phone. But the woman's phone didn't even ring. "A one-time cell phone," he thought. "Damn."

"Well?" Li Chou demanded of the young officer in front of him. "Have you succeeded?" The officer knew very well that Li Chou was not really asking a question but demanding results. The man nodded and held out a diskette that he slid into the D drive of the laptop on Li Chou's desk. With a click of a mouse, a map overlay of Shanghai's streets appeared on the screen. With a second mouse click, a point of light began to blink. The point of light remained in the middle of the screen but the street map overlay was in constant motion identifying the dot's whereabouts.

Li Chou smiled. "How long will it last?"

"It draws power from their bug. As long as their bug's bugging, our bug's bugging their bug. They draw power from the cell phone; we draw power from them."

"Power drawing power," Li Chou thought. He liked that. Then he looked closely at the young man before him. Being a devious man himself, he assumed that this man would also have a hidden side – and more immediately important, a hidden agenda. Li Chou knew that the best way to defeat such agendas was to demand exact details. "How did you mange to bug Captain Chen's bug?"

"Your man saw Chen enter central stores. I called my contact there. He informed me that Captain Chen had requested a bug. Well . . . " the man shrugged, "my friend bugged their bug and gave me the software to follow it."

Li Chou didn't like it. This young man was too clever by half then by half again. He smiled but filed away his concern. He would not nurture potential competition in his ranks.

"Is there a problem, sir?" the man asked.

"No," Li Chou lied easily. "You can leave."

The man waited to get at least a nod of appreciation or a mention of a job well done – but none was forthcoming. He turned and left.

He wasn't brave enough to slam the door.

Li Chou hit the Enlarge icon and immediately the scale of the street map changed. Li Chou checked the street coordinates. There was some sort of Christian temple right there.

He reached for his phone.

Evening prayers began just after sundown. A call to the Bishop of Shanghai confirmed the exact time. Fong had all the cathedral's side doors locked so everyone had to use the main entrance. Just inside the front foyer, Fong had positioned four uniformed cops facing the entrance doors. He and Captain Chen waited outside on the front steps in the hope that a Dalong Fada member would enter the cathedral, see the cops and, as surreptitiously as possible, head right back out.

Fong reached into his pocket and touched the bugged cell phone with the wireless Internet connection he had retrieved from behind the toilet.

"Is this a religious place, sir?" asked Captain Chen.

"Yes, it's a main Catholic church, Xujiahui Cathedral. It was built by the Jesuits. In English they call it St. Ignatius Cathedral."

"We have nothing quite like this in the country."

"No. But with all the beauty out there why would you need it?" Fong checked his watch. It was 8:30 p.m. The service had begun twenty minutes ago. Fong cursed himself for not asking the bishop how long it would go on.

All the people who came to this evening's service had gone past the cops without comment and had stayed for prayers. Shanghanese were usually unfazed by the presence, even the large armed presence, of the police. Fong and Chen watched, but no one had turned around and come back out since the service began.

Li Chou looked at the six CSU detectives in his office. "Keep in cell phone contact with me. I'll guide you. No one is to make any move toward the suspect until I order it. Got that?"

Nods from all six.

"Good. Let's go."

Fong and Captain Chen moved down to the bottom of the cathedral's wide front steps. Time seemed to move two paces forward, one back and one sideways. Then the front doors of the cathedral opened. Fong checked his watch. Evidently evening services were a little longer than an hour. People began to leave the large building. Fong didn't look at the faces. Unless his contact was already inside the cathedral she would arrive soon, looking for a tall white man with what Westerners called black hair but people in the Middle Kingdom knew was really red hair. "We Chinese have black hair," Fong thought. "That's why spoken drama from the West is called Hong Mao Ju, literally red-haired drama."

Then he saw a small middle-aged woman make her way slowly up the steps. She had a slight limp, as if one leg were shorter than the other. Her face was pleasingly calm as she passed by Fong and entered the cathedral. A moment later she re-emerged, shielding her eyes from the remains of the setting sun. She strode down the steps with a quick but unhurried stride.

"Is the bug activated in the phone, Chen?"

"Yes, sir."

"How long will it last?"

"It's hooked into the power supply. Every time the cell phone charges, the bug fills its capacitor. So in theory it could last forever."

Fong just heard this last as he raced to the curb.

The Dalong Fada woman had already crossed the six lanes of traffic and four of bikes on Caoxi Beilu with remarkable ease and was headed directly to the Xujiahui subway station entrance. Fong moved as quickly as he could through the traffic and raced down the stairs to the subway. He dug in his pocket for change, found none, flashed his badge at the ticket-taker then hopped the barrier, to a chorus of complaints from his fellow citizens.

The platform was almost empty as the train pulled out. Fong cussed and was about to turn away in disgust when the last car of the train moved past him revealing the Dalong Fada woman standing patiently on the opposite platform.

Fong ran through the underpass and came up on the platform. He pushed his way through the densely packed crowd ignoring the colourful insults hurled at him and took a position right behind the Dalong Fada woman.

The train came into the station. The Dalong Fada woman stepped in and held onto one of the vertical central posts with her small left hand. Over her right shoulder she had an open red-white-and-blue nylon bag. Fong came up behind her and found a handhold above hers. As the train lurched forward, he slipped the cell phone into her bag then made his way around the pole to look at her.

Instantly, fear bloomed in her eyes. "It's in your bag," Fong said as casually as he could manage.

Her fear receded. She said nothing.

Fong smiled then pushed his way through the throngs in the car, pulled open the door between the cars and stepped into the next car.

He got off at Caoxi Beilu station, took out his cell phone and called Captain Chen. "She on your screen?"

"Yes, sir, I've copied the software to track her onto my PalmPilot and the signal from her cell phone is coming through just fine."

"And our Li Chou?"

Chen laughed aloud, something that Fong had never heard from the man before. He wasn't sure exactly what to make of it.

"Where are you, sir?"

Fong told him.

"Shall I pick you up?"

"Is there any hurry?"

Chen checked the screen of the PalmPilot, "The cell phone's still in motion so I don't think so."

"Fine," said Fong and snapped his phone shut.

Chen looked at the screen of the PalmPilot and then at his cell phone. He thought of Fong's warnings about understanding the politics in the office. Then he thought of his obligation as a husband to Lily and a guardian to Xiao Ming and made a call.

The younger Beijing man picked up and listened for a moment. "This was the wise thing to do." He hung up the phone and turned to the older Beijing man. "He's doing just what we expected."

The older Beijing man nodded, "As Mao said: allow a man to marry and have a child and he is lost to the Revolution." The younger man hadn't heard Mao quoted in quite some time. No one quoted Mao anymore. But it was the wistful tone in the older man's voice that drew his attention.

"Perhaps, but more to the point, they'll lead us right to Xi Luan Tu."

The older man didn't reply; he just looked out the window at the miracle that was modern Shanghai.

Xi Luan Tu saw the limping woman make her way down the alley. He wheeled his barrel of grub pupae through the rusted gate at the back of the old Soviet-style apartment block, where he slept on a basement mattress with twelve others. It was the appointed hour and he'd been waiting there every day at that time for the past two weeks. He watched her limp by, knowing she would make at least three passes before she made her drop.

He hadn't seen her for years. What had once been the slightest imbalance had progressed to a full-fledged limp. She was no longer young. Then again, neither was he. She didn't look in his direction. It surprised him they had sent her. He questioned the wisdom of their choice. Her second time round came quicker than he thought it would. And her third that much quicker again. This time, she paused in front of the seventh garbage can in the row of cans – the assigned one – dropped something wrapped in newspaper into it – then made her way, this time quite slowly, along the alley. Just a good citizen who didn't litter – not an old lover anxious to see her former mate.

Xi Luan Tu wanted to chase after her but knew better. He put a tight metal mesh over the barrel with his grub pupae and locked it in place to an iron ring in the cement wall. Then he took out a cigarette, a snake charmer – he still liked the old brands – and lit up. If she was just a conscientious citizen then he was just a workingman enjoying a butt after a long day's work.

He smoked the harsh thing down to the filter as his eyes scanned the alley for watchers. He smoked a second then lit a third. Lots and lots of people, as there always were, but no one with any seeming interest in either him or the seventh garbage can in the row. He finished his third smoke then headed toward the row of garbage cans.

He executed the pickup with casual precision.

Five minutes later, crouching behind his barrel of grub pupae, he activated the cell phone he'd picked up from the seventh garbage can and made Internet contact – the first of many steps to get him out of Shanghai.

Two minutes after that, Chen contacted Fong, "I believe she delivered the bugged cell phone."

"Do you have an address?"

"Is shrimp dumpling made with shrimp?"

Fong knew that Chen intended this as an affirmative answer to his question although in Shanghai it was extremely unlikely to find shrimp or anything even like shrimp in a shrimp dumpling. "Good, Chen. I'm at Dong Tai Lu in the Old City."

"I'll be right there," and after a brief pause added, "sir."

Fong heard the momentary pause and the slightly pushed end of Chen's speech but didn't know what to make of it.

Xi Luan Tu didn't sleep well that night. He knew he was approaching some very complicated decisions. He wondered about leaving Shanghai. If it were right. Then he wondered about his ability to withstand the pain of torture. Then he wondered at the ingenuity of his brother to arrange all this. Then he wondered at the movement itself that had grown from so few only fifteen years ago into the second strongest force in the People's Republic of China. That thought calmed him and as the dawn crept closer he nodded off.

Chen snored as he slept in the front seat of the car. Fong glanced over at the small screen on the PalmPilot. The bugged phone had not moved all night. Fong assumed that nothing of any real event would happen until the replacement money and the documents for those that Geoff had to burn were finally delivered to Xi Luan Tu. He assumed that the bug would lead them to that hand off. "Then what?" he asked himself. "Then we follow," he answered his own question. But when the question "Why?" popped into his head he simply ducked it. He had absolutely no answer to "Why?" He had, often in the past, successfully followed what Westerners call hunches but he knew were insights. But this was not one of those occasions. He knew, in his heart, that he was following that cell phone because he didn't have anything else to follow. That he had no real clues as to who murdered Geoff. No one with motive. No one who he even needed to interrogate further. Once again it occurred to him that he may have overlooked something obvious, something important.

A car passed by and Fong slid down in his seat. The car turned the far corner of the market and sped away. Fong sat up in his seat. Is it possible that the two Beijing keepers were in that car? No. It's just all this waiting. It's made him jumpy, given him way too much time to think.

And there was lots to think about. Why was the commissioner so quiet in all this? Why was Li Chou at least seemingly being cooperative? Why was there no diplomatic pressure from the Canadians to solve this murder? Or did they think it was a suicide? Had no one even raised the possibility with them that Geoff's death was a murder?"

The PalmPilot beeped. Slowly the street map overlay began to move. He nudged Chen who awoke with a start, as if he had just had a guilty dream. "What time is it, sir?"

"Just before dawn, Captain Chen."

As Fong turned on the ignition and put the car in gear, a phone call was placed. "They're moving, sir," was all the voice said. The elderly Beijing man stretched. The younger Beijing man was surprised how fresh his elderly companion was.

In the predawn cool, Fong and Chen moved carefully through the outdoor street market while the merchants set up for the day. The blip generated by the bug in the cell phone had moved then stopped here in the market. It had been still for a full half-hour. As Fong and Chen moved slowly south through the market toward the blip, others were moving too – toward them.

At the height of the market's morning rush, a peasant woman with a shabby bundle on her back and an awful haircut approached Xi Luan Tu's barrel of grub pupae.

"They're for birds," he said, "not humans."

"Do you think I am such a fool as to eat grubs?" she barked back.

He noticed her southern accent and the exact use of the complex idiom *such a fool*. Then he saw her hands. Dirt-encrusted palms, ragged fingernails – but soft fingers. Not a callus to be seen. Not workers' hands. He shallowed his breathing, ready.

"Are you of the second wave?" he asked.

"I bring the storm," she responded.

"Ah," he said and handed her a large paper sack and began to ladle grub pupae into it.

As she had been instructed, she yelled for him to stop. No one really took note – just another woman trying in vain to get a good bargain at the market.

She unslung her pack, knelt down and opened it. He knelt down beside her with the bag of grubs between them.

In her mind, she'd reviewed the scenario she'd read on yesterday's Internet contact several times. She took a deep breath to clear her head then reached into the grub-filled bag and pulled out a handful of the nascent things. She was surprised they were so slimy but it was their movement inside their casings that almost drew a cry from her throat.

"These are the finest . . . " he began to protest.

She harrumphed and threw her handful of the squirming things at the side of the barrel. He squacked a protest, turned to the barrel while still making a racket and grabbed for the grub pupae. As he did, she shoved the open bag of grubs into her bundle and pulled out another brown paper bag containing the $25,000 in US currency, the passports and the four sets of identification papers that she'd taken from her bundle. He whirled back on her and shouted obscenities, grabbed the bag as if he were taking back his precious grub pupae and told her to get out of his sight.

No one paid them any mind. Joan shouted a particularly colourful obscenity and then stomped away. She felt relieved that the switch had gone so smoothly although mildly disconcerted to think of the hundreds of grub pupae now perhaps loose in her pack.

She moved quickly, looking for the way out – back to her life in Hong Kong.

She passed out of the grub-seller section of the market and turned the corner. Immediately she was assailed by the sound of thousands of birds. Everywhere she looked, wrens, finches, canaries and kingfishers perched in bamboo cages that were piled by the walls of the buildings – sometimes four or five stories high.

She leaned back to get a better look and felt something hard and cold against her neck. A voice she thought she recognized said, "Don't make a fuss. We don't want to hurt you."

Chen was surprised when Fong put his gun to the nape of the neck of the peasant woman with the bad haircut, who had done nothing but try to buy some grub pupae. But he wasn't surprised to see, out of the corner of his eye, the two Beijing men running, followed by a dozen federal cops all heading right for the tall middle-aged man standing behind the barrel of live grub pupae.

Xi Luan Tu saw it all happen before him and executed the escape plan he'd worked out months ago. He grabbed the brown paper bag with the money, ID and passports, patted his pocket once to assure himself he still had the cell phone, kicked over his barrel of grub pupae then charged around the corner and threw himself right at the mountain of fragile bamboo birdcages. Instantly, hundreds of the delicately balanced things crashed to the ground and split open – freeing their tiny captives. Amidst the screams of their owners, the birds moved as one living thing, claimed their freedom then headed directly for the mass of grub pupae on the ground. The shouts of anger and the hundreds of dive-bombing birds gave Xi Luan Tu enough cover to head toward the warrens.

A volley of gunshots cut through the mayhem. A window shattered. An old man screamed in pain. Xi Luan Tu sped down the alleyway that accessed the warrens. As he made the last turn, he slipped and crashed to the pavement. He heard the skip of bullets off pavement all around him. When he regained his feet, a sharp pain on the outside of his left thigh almost threw him back to the ground. Then he heard a bullet splat into the alley wall beside his head and he forgot about the pain in his thigh or the blood that was flowing freely down his leg and pooling in his sock. He summoned all his strength and raced toward the safety of the warrens.

On the first gunshot, Fong grabbed the peasant woman with the bundle and shoved her into the safety of a doorway. More shots. Birds screeched, people screamed.

"Do you know who I am?" Fong hissed.

Joan nodded.

For a moment, Fong didn't know what to do then he said, "Do you trust me?"

Joan didn't move.

"Well, here are your choices. You trust me and help me or I hand you over to the federal officers who will arrest you for treason."

Joan looked at Fong. "If you put it that way . . . "

The Beijing men stood behind a stall that sold polished drift-wood about halfway between Fong and the alley entrance to the warrens. The younger Beijing man barked orders to the local militia he had stationed strategically in the Old City. He paced as they began evacuating buildings and then entered the warrens from four different access points. The older Beijing man stood patiently to one side and allowed his fingers to trace the pleasing curve of one of the polished pieces . . . and he watched. He assumed Xi Luan Tu had a fifty-fifty chance of avoiding the troops in the warrens. But the Dalong Fada leader had no chance of avoiding Fong because of the bug in the cell phone – so the older Beijing man waited for Fong, his uncomely Captain Chen and the peasant woman with the awful haircut to make their move. Their move would betray Xi Tuan Lu's whereabouts. His finger snagged as a splinter of wood entered a full two inches into his right ring finger. He didn't wince but rather slowly backed his finger off the splinter. A thin line of blood dripped down his finger and pooled in his palm.

Fong turned to Chen, "Captain Chen, Joan Shui. Joan Shui, Captain Chen."

Chen didn't know what to do, whether he should shake hands or what. Before he could make up his mind, Fong asked, "We still have him?" Chen showed him the PalmPilot with the street overlays. "Not all that useful with Xi Luan Tu underground in the warrens."

"We'll have to follow the best we can. I think it's time to throw our friends off the track, don't you, Captain Chen?"

Chen hesitated for a moment as if he were unsure of the meaning of Fong's question. Fong saw it and a shiver of fear went up his spine. Chen smiled and took out his cell phone. He punched in 555 555 555 1, listened for a tone, got it, then punched the pound key twice. Then he flipped his cell phone shut and said, "Problem turned into opportunity, sir."

Li Chou had heard the shots and screams from the market. The blip on his laptop began to move like someone running then stopped. He had his men in position and was about to give them directions when all of a sudden the street map overlay on his receiver began to move at tremendous speed. "Hold on," he shouted into his cell phone. Finally the street map slowed then suddenly stopped. Li Chou looked at the thing. Shook it. The blip didn't move. He hit the Enlarge button to get an exact address then dialled the snitch in central stores. He quickly told the man what had happened.

The man really didn't know what to make of Li Chou's information but asked, "The blip is stable now?"

"Yes."

"And you can identify the cross streets?"

"Yes."

"Well, that's where the bug must be."

Li Chou contacted his men on his cell phone and shouted orders to them, hit the siren, U-turned across eight lanes of traffic and sped toward the arrest that he knew would send Zhong Fong back to the wasteland west of the Wall.

While Li Chou's siren pierced the din of Shanghai's constant traffic jam, the young Beijing man stayed above-ground and on a makeshift map charted the unsteady progress of his troops in the warrens. Beside him, the older Beijing man kept his eyes on Fong, Chen and the peasant woman, who was with them now.

"Money and passports and ID papers," Joan answered Fong's question. "I brought him all those things. Maybe you should arrest me."

"Maybe I will," said Fong.

Joan looked at the blip on the PalmPilot. "How did you bug him?"

"It's in the cell phone I brought him."

"Do you know who he is, Zhong Fong?"

Fong nodded but said nothing. The blip had stopped moving. He looked at Chen who nodded. Then they moved quickly.

The older Beijing man sat up straight and tapped the younger Beijing man. He pointed at Fong and Chen and the peasant woman who were running across the alley not twenty yards ahead of them.

Li Chou whispered directions into his radio transmitter. His men responded with whispered affirmatives when they had reached their assigned positions around the Park Regent Hotel in the fashionable embassy district in the south end of the city. Four of the six had reported. He awaited the last two before he made his move.

The tunnels got steeper and steeper while Fong, Chen and Shui made their way deeper and deeper into the heart of the warrens. Chen guided them as best he could by the blip on the screen of the PalmPilot. Fong knew the ins and outs of most of Shanghai, but this underground world was foreign to him. As a child, he'd ventured into the warrens only a few times. Although he was never wealthy, Fong's family had controlled night-soil collection throughout the Old City and he had some standing as a part of the family's age-old business. The warrens were for those who had nothing. Not people like him. It was their domain, not his. The last time he'd gone down there he was twelve years old. He'd been robbed, beaten and only escaped worse through the unexpected kindness of one of the older ruffians.

They passed by filthy mattresses on the wet ground and other evidence of human habitation. The blip had not moved for over ten minutes. Xi Luan Tu must have gone to ground. On occasion, the shouts of the militiamen echoed to them from a distance, but even these thinned out in the last few minutes. Twice Fong had put his hand up for them to stop and crept back to see if they were being followed. He was convinced that he'd heard footsteps but could not find anyone on their tail.

They'd reached a turn in the tunnel. To their right the tunnel widened and headed toward the river. Directly in front of them was an almost sheer wall of rock. Chen put his fingers to his lips, looked at the blip then signalled that he was confused. Fong looked at the screen. It indicated straight ahead – somehow on the other side of the rock face, not down the tunnel. Fong was about to cuss all technology when he saw a wet sheen on the rock face. A sheen he recognized all too well. He reached up and touched the sticky slickness of fresh blood.

The two Beijing men stood in the darkness of the tunnel and took out their firearms. Modern, German, lethal.

Li Chou got the "In place!" from the last of his men. He took a breath. Referred one last time to the laptop. The blip had not moved. He counted to ten then yelled, "Now."

Climbing the rock face proved easier than it looked. Well-concealed but numerous handholds and footholds had been cut into the rock at appropriate intervals. This was evidently a much-travelled route. At the very top of the rock face was a small opening. Fong led; Joan and Chen followed. The opening narrowed so that even someone as slender as Fong had to squeeze to get through. But once through, a large tunnel travelled for ten yards then opened into a substantial cave. Along the walls of the cave were dozens of large barrels. Chen consulted the PalmPilot then pointed to a large barrel stencilled in white paint with: **TO BE DELIVERED TO HU FAT CHOI SPADINA ROAD TORONTO CANADA.**

The raid on the Park Regent Hotel's coffee shop went off like clockwork. Li Chou's men scared the shit out of all eight customers, the two cooks and the young skimpily clad waitress. Li Chou then consulted his laptop and pointed beneath a table at the far side of the restaurant. When he threw back the white tablecloth, the man beneath yelped a complaint.

Chen pried the barrel's upper ring loose and all the slats fell to the floor, revealing the calmly seated figure of Xi Luan Tu.

Li Chou lifted Shrug and Knock in one angry sweep from beneath the table, then shook him. The electronic button that fell from his coat hit the table then bounced to the floor and rolled into a corner. On Li Chou's laptop the street map overlay moved ever so slightly to indicate the movement.

Li Chou's face was hot, angry and naturally, fat.

Fong held out a hand to Xi Luan Tu. The man took it and rose to his full height. Fong locked eyes with him.

"Take your hands off him, Traitor Zhong!"

Fong turned. There in the mouth of the cave stood the younger Beijing man, his gun pointed right at Xi Luan Tu's head.

Joan took a step in front of Xi Luan Tu.

"Bad move, peasant girl," said the younger Beijing man, cocked his gun and pulled the trigger.

Fong threw himself at Joan and covered her prone body with his.

The sound of the gunshot in the cave was incredibly loud. Joan let out a small whimper. The echo of the shot slowly faded and faded and faded until all that remained was a profound silence.

One by one, Fong, Joan and Chen lifted their heads, then stared at the mouth of the cave. The younger Beijing man's body slumped against the wall, a large exit wound in his forehead. Slowly, from the tunnel darkness, the elder Beijing man emerged with a firearm in his hand. He looked at the body of the younger Beijing man then turned to Fong, "We need to talk."

Twenty minutes later, they were in a safe house just across the Huangpo River. It was the same safe house where the elder Beijing man conducted the counterterrorism seminar on the night that Geoffrey Hyland had been murdered.

"So who goes first?" asked Fong.

"Goes?" the older Beijing man asked.

"Yes. Who explains their actions first?"

"You, Fong," said the older Beijing man.

"Sure," said Fong noting there was none of that Traitor Zhong stuff. "I figured out that Geoff had more information."

"As I hoped you would."

"Fine. It led me to a cell phone that I was to deliver to a contact that would bring it to Xi Luan Tu. I bugged the phone and followed it."

"Why?"

Fong lied smoothly, "To find out if any of this bullshit has anything to do with Mr. Hyland's murder."

"Ah," said the older Beijing man.

"Yeah, ah. Your turn now," said Fong. The older Beijing man nodded. "Start with how you managed to follow me?"

"We knew you were a talent, Detective Zhong. We assumed you would succeed. We put you under surveillance. It took sixteen watchers but was simple really. Does that answer your question?"

Fong didn't know if that answer was okay or not, but before he could ask another question the older Beijing man turned to Joan, "How about you, young lady? Why are you in Shanghai?"

Joan took a moment, reached up to straighten her hair only to realize that she no longer had enough hair to need straightening and said, "Beijing needs to be kept in check. There is no opposition in this country now that Hong Kong has been taken over. Only Dalong Fada can offer that opposition."

To Fong's surprise, the older Beijing man slowly nodded

his agreement. Then he sat heavily and began to talk.

Fong usually had little time or sympathy for the views from the past. The mantle of righteousness taken on by the elders of China had deeply soured his response to them. But this was different. This man had clearly crossed the line. And what came out of his mouth was as revolutionary as Fong had heard in some time. The man laid out the need for a countervailing force to the power of Beijing, which was, like Joan, what he saw in Dalong Fada. He then said, "I think the religious side of Dalong Fada is stupid and potentially, like all religious movements, dangerous. But better a Chinese solution than a foreign one because, make no mistake, the West is anxious to put a stop to any recklessness coming out of China. But you must also understand that there will never be democracy in this country." He looked to Fong, then to Chen, then to Joan and finally to Xi Luan Tu. No one deigned to respond to that. "It's really quite simple. At base level this is all about survival. We need to assure the steady supply of food for our people. In a city like Shanghai where there are eighteen million people and little or no refrigeration. The very task of getting food, before it spoils, to the people is daunting. Any disruption would cause chaos. And we all know that chaos must be avoided at all cost." This last met with at least some acceptance in the room.

"So you saved Xi Luan Tu to guarantee a real opposition to the chairman of the Chinese Communist Party?" asked Fong.

The man nodded. "Twenty-five-million followers of Dalong Fada qualify as a real opposition, wouldn't you say?"

Joan watched the man with the basic wariness that all Hong Kong residents felt toward the powers in Beijing.

"But it's the only form of democracy we're ready for in the Middle Kingdom at this time. It's a crucial small step, like opening some free markets and allowing freedom of movement for most people within the country. Both freedoms are much more widespread than they were only ten years ago, but they aren't absolute. How could they be and have us avoid chaos? Can you imagine the eighteen million people in this city suddenly all forced to pay for the spaces that they live in? Can you imagine them trying to reshuffle almost sixty years of price control into a completely open market?"

Fong nodded, thinking back to the insider's offer sheet in his desk in his bedroom.

The elderly Beijing man coughed into his hand then continued, "It would lead to riots and then would come Revolution. And make no mistake, before that Revolution came to a conclusion, millions of Chinese would lose their lives, most from starvation. I needn't add that outsiders would soon take advantage of our weakness and we would be back where we were at the beginning of the twentieth century with foreigners controlling our country."

Fong thought that through. He agreed with most of it. "What about Mr. Hyland?"

"What about him?"

"Did you or your younger half have him murdered?"

The older Beijing man shook his head slowly then opened a portfolio that he withdrew from the desk. From the portfolio he removed twelve eight-by-ten photographs and lined them up on the desk.

They showed Geoff arrested, tried for treason, disgraced in front of a large crowd, then put on an airplane in chains. Once again, the faked photos were expertly done. If Fong hadn't seen Geoff hanging from that rope he could well believe that this was a real account of what had happened to his old rival. "This was Beijing's intent. They didn't care about Mr. Hyland. All they wanted from him was to lead them to Xi Luan Tu. Which is exactly what you did for us, Zhong Fong. But their intent and mine were not the same. I wanted to be led to Xi Luan Tu to tell him that he has much support in high circles, not for his religious practices which, as I mentioned, I find obscene, but for the very practical need for political ballast in the People's Republic of China. And now you have led me to him and now he has heard what I have to say."

Xi Luan Tu nodded, as if engaged for the first time in the conversation. Then he got to his feet and headed toward the door.

Joan leapt up and said, "We need to get you out of Shanghai. That's what the money and the Internet access were for."

For the first time, Xi Luan Tu spoke, "That's what they were for, for you Ms. Shui, and I thank you for your efforts. I thank all of you. But I am not leaving Shanghai. I cannot leave Shanghai." Fong began to protest but Xi Luan Tu cut him off, "Do you know a writer named Alan Paton, Zhong Fong?"

Fong shook his head.

"He was a world-renown South African novelist who wrote at great length against the sins of his countrymen and the Apartheid regime. Over and over again, reporters from outside South Africa would ask him why he didn't leave. Do you know what he answered?" He waited for a response but no one spoke. Finally Xi Luan Tu said, "Mr. Paton said that a man without a country is not a man. All of us in this room know that Shanghai is like a country. In fact, it is bigger than many countries. Shanghai is my country. I will not leave it. Again I thank all of you for your efforts. I really do. But now I must leave you. I have no doubt we will all meet again."

"Mr. Xi?"

"Yes, Captain Chen?"

"You'd better give me that phone." Xi Luan Tu gave it to Chen who quickly removed the faceplate and extracted the small electronic bug. For a moment he held it in his hand then dropped it to the floor and stomped on it. The thing flattened without a sound. Then Chen held out the phone to Xi Luan Tu, who took it and headed toward the door. No one made a move to stop him and he did not hesitate in his going.

It left the four of them alone in the safe house – looking at each other. It was Chen who finally broke the silence, "So we are back to a straightforward murder investigation."

The older Beijing man nodded.

"And you and yours didn't murder Mr. Hyland?" Fong asked the Beijing man again.

The Beijing man just pointed to the object-lesson photos. "We didn't want him killed. We wanted him to be an example to foreigners who meddle in the affairs of our country."

"Why doesn't Beijing know about you?" Fong asked.

"Beijing runs just like the rest of China – like the rest of humanity. It survives in boxes. Compartments. It's how we live our lives. Not everything influences everything else. Our work doesn't necessarily influence our politics. Our politics don't necessarily influence our home lives . . ." He stopped and looked at Fong, "What?"

"Compartments. Work not necessarily influencing our home lives – or our love lives."

"What are you talking about, Fong?" asked Joan.

"Are you heading back to Hong Kong right away?"

"I don't know . . ."

"I could really use a woman's eyes to help me on this." He didn't wait for her response but turned to Chen. "Remember the woman I arrested in the bar for murdering her boss?"

"You mean for murdering the man she loved?"

Fong looked hard at Chen. "Yes, that is what I mean, Captain Chen. Arrange for Ms. Shui and me to see her – the woman who killed the man she loved."

"To check on something?"

"Yes, Captain Chen, to check on something I'm pretty sure I overlooked."

"Zhong Fong." It was the elderly Beijing man. "I would

appreciate the courtesy of you sharing the results of your investigations with me."

"Why?"

"Politics is just an attempt to understand the workings of the human heart. If your findings increase my knowledge of that, then I can be of more help to our people."

Fong nodded. "What's your name, sir?"

"Sheng."

Sheng was not a name you heard often. It literally meant "in the year of peace." Fong thought, "What a good name for a man. Yet this man had shot his partner without a word of warning." Fong took another look at the man. The man stood very still as if he understood Fong's thoughts. "Peace in a dangerous world at times requires action – complicated action," Fong said. The man nodded. "Well, where can I find you, Sheng?"

"I'll be here in this house for at least a week."

CHAPTER FIFTEEN

WITH A MURDERESS

Visitation rights don't exist in Chinese jails. So when Fong, through Captain Chen, demanded access to the woman who murdered the man she loved, the penal system first had to find the woman then arrange how the meeting could take place. While the authorities worked things out, Fong tried to find a transcript of the woman's trial. But despite his best efforts he couldn't even find a record of the verdict. Fong had no doubt she had been found guilty but access to court records, like jail visitations in the People's Republic of China, are not guaranteed.

The call finally came through. A place. A time.

The woman who murdered the man she loved sat quietly on a small three-legged bamboo stool and did not rise when Fong and Joan Shui entered the dank room. When the jailor began to close the door, Fong turned to him, "Don't."

The woman who murdered the man she loved sat looking at her hands. Fong looked at them too. Her slender fingers were now capped by ragged bitten nails. Only the false nail of her right ring finger remained from her fashionable French manicure. She pushed up the sleeves of her prison blouse and lifted her head. Immediately she saw the way he was looking at her. "Wait till they cut off my hair, then I'll really be a treat to look

at. Like her," she said pointing to Joan, "a real fashion statement."

Fong had actually been surprised that they hadn't cut off
the woman's hair. It was pretty much common practice. They
claimed it was to keep down the lice but Fong knew otherwise.
Like so much of prison life it was to break down any sense of
anyone being special, being other than a prisoner at the total
behest of the state.

"You've been in prison," she said. It was a statement not a
question.

Fong nodded. "This woman knew that I had been in love.
Now she knows that I have been in prison," he thought. He
looked more closely at her. But she looked away saying,
"Don't."

He began to apologize then decided against it. Beauty was
to be shared. It was just one of the many talents. Fu Tsong had
told him that, then quoted some parable or something from the
West's Bible about hiding money under apple carts or some
such nonsense. As with so many things from that most ques-
tionable of books, Fong had no idea what it meant – if in fact it
meant anything.

"Why are you here, Detective Zhong?" she asked. But he
heard the waver in her voice. The inherent pause. The uncer-
tainty that prison had already implanted in her.

"How long is your sentence?"

"Does it matter?"

"Yes. As someone who has been in a place like this, yes, it
matters. On that, trust me."

"Well, they haven't decided yet."

"When are they going to decide?"

She made a sound that in the time before the murder would
no doubt have been called a laugh. Now, prison had modified
the sound and it was little different than the sound made to
clear the throat before spitting up phlegm.

Fong made himself go over the timeline. The murder had taken place only ten days ago so it was possible that she would be sentenced shortly but it was not likely. If they were going to sentence her it should have happened by now. If they were going to execute her he wouldn't have been allowed to see her. Likely she would be imprisoned as long as the authorities thought it useful. That could be as little as three years or as long as her life.

"What are you doing here, Detective Zhong?" she asked again.

"I want to talk to you."

"Well, that's good because if you came here to fuck me that could prove above even your ingenuity." She looked at Joan Shui for a second then said, "Sorry."

"Don't be," Joan said.

"Have you got a cigarette?"

"Sorry," said Joan.

"I do," said Fong.

He had brought cigarettes for precisely this situation but now he hesitated. He didn't want to bribe her to talk to him. He wanted her to want to talk to him.

The woman who had murdered the man she loved lifted her left buttock and farted loudly. She waved her hand in the air in front of her to dissipate the odour. "Sorry, but the food in here isn't exactly agreeing with my gastric system."

Fong smiled. Then took the smile off his face. "Why am I at such a loss here?" he asked himself. Before he completed the question he shouted the answer at himself in the recesses of his head, "Because, jerk, you don't know why you're here." He reached into his shirt pocket, tapped out a Kent and held it out to her.

She reached for it, careful not to touch the skin of his fingers or hand. She put the cigarette between her lips. It was only then that he noticed they were bruised.

"Did someone hit you?"

"You've been in prison before, right? People get hit in prison. I need a light."

He struck a stick match on the floor and held it up to her. The flaring of the match touched moments of light to the skin of her face. Little licks of beauty.

She breathed out a thin line of smoke just past Fong's left ear. Before he could stop himself he breathed in her smoke.

"You smoked too. Interesting," she said. "Why not join me?"

Fong hadn't smoked since he'd killed the assassin Loa Wei Fen in the construction site in the Pudong almost seven years ago, but he was direly tempted to break his smoke fast. But he didn't. "If they hit you again, get word to me and I'll put a stop to it."

Again she made the sound that only a few weeks ago must have been a laugh but now sounded like something very different. "Are you really capable of doing that?" she said.

Fong didn't answer. He didn't know if he could control events within a prison. He'd never tried.

"It's better to be hit than raped," she said.

Fong found himself nodding although he didn't want to.

She lifted her head, took the cigarette from her lips and stared into his eyes. "Why are you here? Again I ask."

"To try and understand."

"Understand what?"

"Understand how you could kill the man you loved," said Joan Shui.

"Is that really what you want to know?" she asked Fong. He nodded. The woman who killed the man she loved opened her mouth to answer then put her face in her hands. For a moment Fong thought she was going to cry. But she didn't. "Answer your own question, Detective. You've loved, you've been in prison, maybe you've even killed."

Fong looked away. The desire to get out of that room roared up from his depths. This woman somehow knew him. How? But he needed her. The simple Chinese word *long*, dragon, came up to his lips. Dragons always guarded treasure. They had to be defeated to gain the knowledge – or wooed.

"How did you first meet Mr. Clayton?"

"How do you think?" Her voice was harsh. Suddenly the practised whore.

"You were a hired date for him?" Joan asked, careful to keep any annoyance out of her voice.

"I was given to him by a Chinese client. I was there in his hotel room when he returned from a night of drinking. Naked. Waiting. All greased up and ready to go." She noticed Fong wince at that last. "Nothing to be embarrassed about, Detective Zhong. Ready to go because I didn't want to get pregnant. Greased up because it wasn't likely that I'd produce much lather at the possibility of fucking this Long Nose or any Long Nose for that matter. Or so I thought. Can I have another smoke?"

He gave her the pack and was about to give her the matches then remembered that it was forbidden. He struck a match and held it out. She leaned forward and cupped his hands.

Then held them.

Over the flame, amidst the veil of her cigarette smoke, he saw her more clearly. Her eyes were the eyes of a ghost.

He made sure his voice was calm before he spoke, "So you slept with Mr. Clayton?"

"No, Detective Zhong, I didn't sleep with him. Whores aren't paid to sleep with clients."

Fong nodded.

Then a single line of tears emerged from the corner of her right eye and fell straight to the floor. "He bought me breakfast."

The phrase was so simple but it carried so much weight. Somehow she knew that if he hadn't bought her breakfast they would never have started what ended with him dead and her in this awful place.

For a moment he wanted to ask if the breakfast was good. But he knew the answer to the question. The food had tasted as exquisite as food could taste. The sun had been as brilliant as the sun can shine – and the world seemed gracious, open and full of hope. Fong knew that.

Sensing the momentum slip, Joan asked, "When did you see him next?"

"He drove me home and gave me money to rent a hotel room. It was the first time I ever had a room to myself. I almost didn't know what to do with all that space."

"Did he come by that night?" asked Joan.

"No. Not for a week."

"Why?"

"He told me that he wanted to be sure."

"Sure of what?" asked Fong.

"Oh, fucking hell, sure that the breakfast was good, sure that I was a woman, sure that Korea is a peninsula of idiots, what do you think he wanted to be sure of?"

Fong took a breath. "Sure that he cared for you."

"Whites don't come back again if they only care about a Chinese girl."

"No, they don't." Fong considered lighting up but forced that thought out of his head. "So he loved you?"

She looked away. "That word sounds silly coming out of your mouth."

"I'm sorry."

"Have you been so hurt by love that love is now a joke to you, Detective Zhong?"

"No . . ."

"Then what?"

"Doesn't it take longer to fall in love than . . . "

"Then one fuck fest? Is that what you're asking?"

He was, but he knew the answer to that. He had fallen hopelessly in love with Fu Tsong within the first fifteen minutes of her saying hello to him. They hadn't even touched. They'd hardly exchanged words. It sounded foolish – but he knew it was true.

"So what happened to your love?"

She began to answer but she was crying. Big sobs came from a place very deep in her. Tears fell on her cigarette. The thing hissed.

"Like a dragon," Fong thought. But he said nothing. He sat and watched waves of anguish take the woman who murdered the man she loved down down down into places of despair that had yet to be named. A place where only ghosts lived.

And as he watched he knew both the question he needed to ask and the answer to his question. He had known it before he came to this small prison room. Question: Can love kill? Answer: No, but things that begin with love can end in murder.

He looked to Joan who looked away, clearly trying to stop herself from crying.

"Are you all right?" Fong asked as he got into his car beside Joan.

"Yes. I'm fine. In fact, I'm better for having seen that."

"Really?"

"Yes. Where to?"

Fong took a moment and then replied, "To those who loved Geoff."

She nodded slowly and sat back. While Fong made his way through the densely tangled traffic, Joan soaked in the great city. As they drove, a small smile came to her face. Shanghai flaunted itself – like a young woman in her first sexy dress – as if it were a thing newly made and proud – and finally open for public viewing.

CHAPTER SIXTEEN

DA WEI

D a Wei, Geoff's homely translator, indicated that Fong and Joan Shui should sit at the small table in the cubicle that passed as her room at the Shanghai Theatre Academy. They did.

Ignoring Joan, Da Wei said, "I've been expecting you, Detective Zhong."

"Have you?"

She stopped and stared at him. "I said as much."

"You did," he said nodding. It startled Fong to realize that they were speaking English.

"Your English is very good, Detective Zhong."

"Thank you, but not nearly as good as yours, Da Wei."

She nodded and poured tea from a large Thermos into the empty glass jars on the table. The tepid-coloured liquid swirled around the slender languid leaves of the tea that stood on the bottom of the jars, waving like sea plants.

He thanked her. She poured some for herself and sat directly opposite him.

He tasted the dark earthiness of the *cha* and knew that it was a special treat for Da Wei to serve such an exotic blend. He was about to comment on it when she said, "I was very fond of your wife, Fu Tsong. She was a great, great actress, a true artist. I was honoured to help her prepare her English for . . . " Her voice ended as if somehow a finger had been placed over a stop.

He looked at her. So she had prepared Fu Tsong's English for the production she had never gotten to do with Geoff in Vancouver.

"I'm sorry," she said, "it's inexcusable of me to mention such things."

Fong looked away. A futon was folded to one side and a night table stood beside it. On the night table were small mementoes from her life. A set of tiny bells aligned between two wooden poles, an ornamental teapot in the shape of a dragon, three oblong, flat, polished blood stones from the Yangtze River and a round black rubber disk of some sort with a logo of a sporting team on it. Fong couldn't identify either the disk or the logo. But that didn't concern him now. Something about the way the objects were arrayed on the table did. It was as if there was a missing item – maybe two small missing items.

He looked at Da Wei then at the walls of the cubicle. Standard-issue pictures of a southern water town, two posters from plays she'd worked on at the theatre academy, a "new school" rendition of a classical pastoral scene executed in watercolours on a hanging scroll.

Again something missing. The visual aesthetic of the room was consistent, consistent, consistent, then absent.

Then he noticed a slight area of brightness peeking out from behind the scroll painting. It was like the section of wall in his room that at one time had been covered by Lily's antique frescoed sculpture. He got up and moved the scroll painting aside. An eight-by-ten-inch rectangle showed brighter on the wall than the surrounding area. Da Wei's cubicle was extremely clean but uncovered walls collected dirt in Shanghai; the pollution is inescapable. So an area that was covered then uncovered would show bright against the rest of the wall.

Fong looked from the eight-by-ten brightness to the round

black rubber disk with the logo on Da Wei's night table.

Then he looked at the theatre posters. "Don't you have any posters from the shows you worked on with Mr. Hyland?"

"I do. Several."

"May I see them?"

"They're in communal storage. You may notice that I have no closet space here."

Fong nodded and said, "Ah," then he glanced at the blank brightness on the wall again. He crossed over and picked up the rubber object from Da Wei's night table. He held it close to read the writing on the logo. "What's a Canuck?" he asked.

"A hockey player from Vancouver, I believe. That's called a puck. Do you know about hockey, Detective Zhong?"

No, he didn't, but he knew about someone who did. He remembered Geoff's reference on the CD-ROM and an incident years ago when Geoff was directing in Shanghai and frantically tried to find a newspaper that would tell him who won the Larry Cup – or Gerty Cup – some kind of hockey cup. "So Mr. Hyland gave you the puck as a souvenir?"

She nodded. Then poured herself more tea and hid her face in the mist from her cup.

"Not a particularly romantic gift, wouldn't you say?"

"I don't understand you, Detective Zhong."

"Should we speak in the Common Tongue? Would that help you understand me?"

She was instantly on her feet, no doubt about to demand he leave her room, but before she could speak, Fong pulled down the scroll painting and pointed at the eight-by-ten inch brightness on the wall. "So was this where you kept Mr. Hyland's picture?" She stared at him. Her mouth was open, revealing cracked teeth. "Did he sign it for you? Maybe with the words: *With all my love, Geoff?*"

"No," she said and sat heavily. "Not those words. '*I couldn't do it without you, Da Wei*' it said."

"You cared for him," Fong said.

She nodded slowly.

"But he didn't reciprocate your affection? Is reciprocate the right word?"

"You know it is," she snapped. Then she took a deep breath and let her air out slowly. "No, Detective Zhong, he did not reciprocate. I was not blessed with . . . " The words failed her. She just shook her head and tears began to well in her round eyes as she contemplated the whole injustice of beauty. "I am not beautiful like your wife or Yue Feng."

Fong stood very still. "Mr. Hyland was seeing Yue Feng, the actress who plays Ophelia?"

"Now it is I who must ask about word selection. What do you mean by 'was seeing'?" She reverted to Mandarin. "Do you mean being attracted to – yes. Touching her backstage – yes. Having her in his rooms – yes. Fucking her – that, not having been there, I wouldn't know." She smiled wanly. "If you follow my meaning, Detective Zhong."

"I do." He got to his feet. "Have you got a passport, Da Wei?"

"Yes."

"I'll need to hold that for you."

She balked for a moment then opened a small drawer in the table and handed over her way out of the Middle Kingdom.

CHAPTER SEVENTEEN

FOR LOVE

Once again the day's heat had decided to spend the night inside the old theatre. While the rest of Shanghai had a momentary respite, the air inside the theatre was sultry, almost hazy in its dampness.

"You wanted to see us?" The voice came from the darkness at the back of the theatre.

"Another voice from the darkness," Fong thought but he said nothing.

"I said, you wanted to see us?" The voice was demanding, angry. It belonged to Ho Tu Pei, the actor who played Laertes.

Fong stood on the slanted stage platform from which the naked Hamlet began his nightly voyage. His back was to the house. Fong assumed the "us" in Laertes' repeated question meant that he had brought along the actress Yue Feng, who played Ophelia, as Fong had requested. Good.

Fong continued to face upstage and raised his hand. Slowly a hangman's noose descended from the flies. Fong reached up and took the noose in his hands. Then he turned to the darkened auditorium where he knew Laertes and Ophelia were watching him. "So once I figured out that this all had to do with love – not nefarious plots," Fong said, "the only thing that confused me was how to get the noose over Geoff's head then tighten it around his neck – and, of course, keep it there." Fong took a few steps stage left then turned, "Do you mind if I call you by your character names? I'm sorry but that's the way I think of you both. Is that okay with you two?" He didn't wait for an answer. "So my problem wasn't how to yank Geoff off the ground – counterweights answered that. But, as I said, that wasn't my problem. My problem was: how did you manage to get the rope around Geoff's neck. Mr. Hyland is a white man – well it's not his colour that's the issue here but the height that often accompanies a white man's skin. Geoff was just over six foot two inches tall – so you see my problem? I mean how does a five-foot-six-inch Chinese man – or a five-foot-two-inch Chinese woman – manage to get a noose around a six-foot-two-inch white man's neck – who was not drugged or drunk. You follow me so far?"

Again Fong didn't wait for an answer.

"Then I thought about that chair by the pinrail. At first I thought it was there for actors to rest on or for the flyman to loaf on between cues. But the flyman was a proud professional, as he told me many times, and would not put up with actors in his territory or in any way slack off while on duty – therefore he had no need for a chair.

"So what was the chair doing there? Ms. Shui, would you bring out the offending chair, please."

Joan emerged from the stage-left wings carrying the chair.

"Put it there, would you, thanks. Now would you hold the noose for me? Thanks."

Fong indicated the chair, "Ophelia, this is for you."

"For what?" Her voice was husky with anger.

"Ah." Fong paused. "Just do me the favour of sitting in the chair, would you?"

Slowly Ophelia climbed the stairs to the stage. As she did, Joan retreated to the darkness upstage. Fong pointed to the chair. Ophelia sat in it. She was slender and young – Fong could see how some could see her as attractive – a poor substitute for Fu Tsong, but a substitute in the eyes of some – Geoff's, for example.

"Could you loosen your hair, please?" Fong said.

She looked at him then unknotted her hair. It fell like a black silken curtain almost to the floor – very much like Fu Tsong's had.

Fong closed his eyes for a moment. When he opened them, he saw that Ophelia dangled the clip that had kept her hair in place from the index finger of her left hand. He nodded slowly.

"So you two, you and Mr. Hyland, had just been together, had it off, brought on the clouds and rain – you pick. We can trace your contraceptive to stains on Mr. Hyland's clothing."

Fong sensed Captain Chen staring at him from the pinrail and realized that he had been shouting at the girl. He lowered his voice, "You had managed it, I assume, in his room, and your boyfriend didn't even know – or so Geoff thought. He never really understood us, did he? He never understood our patience, our willingness to wait for revenge.

"So you were done and the night was still young. Couldn't stay in his room; couldn't chance being spotted by a key lady coming out of Geoff's room; at least not that night. But you and Geoff wanted more time and privacy. Now where could you find that amidst the eighteen million of us who live in this town? In the theatre, of course. Geoff surely had a key. It was late so no one else would be there. Now to go back a bit, you must have left Geoff's room first. Leaving together would definitely have caught someone's attention – you know how nosey we Shanghanese are – especially when one of our women is with one of their men, no? So you leave and, using Geoff's key, you enter the theatre through the pinrail door, there. But, oh yes, you didn't just let yourself in – did you – this hanging took two, didn't it?"

She began to get up from the chair but Fong's crisp, "I

wouldn't do that," made her rethink standing up. "Good," Fong said taking a step away from her. Then he began again. "So you let Laertes into the theatre and he hid behind the pinrail door – with the noose of course. Would you please, Captain Chen?" Fong waited as Chen took the noose and got into place behind the door. Fong surveyed the situation then crossed downstage and addressed the darkness, "Playing Laertes gave you lots of time to watch the flyman and figure out what he does. After all, Laertes is in the whole play but he's hardly ever onstage. You do get to wait in the wings and watch the most famous speeches in Shakespeare performed by Hamlet; that must have been a real treat for you. But that's not the point. The flyman and his counterweights are the point."

"At any rate, Laertes hides with the noose and you, dear Ophelia, position this chair with its back to the pinrail door. You sit on the chair and when you hear Geoff enter you lean forward, your elbows almost on your knees, and pull your hair to one side and forward to reveal the nape of your neck."

"Do it!" Fong barked.

She did.

The simple line of her neck was exquisite.

"Geoff stepped forward like this, didn't he, and he leaned over to kiss the nape of your neck like this, didn't he?"

Ophelia shuddered and began to cry. Her slender body suddenly taken by tremours.

"Then Laertes leapt out of his hiding place behind the door and while Mr. Hyland was bent over you he slipped the rope around Geoff's neck. Captain Chen."

Chen raced forward and looped the noose over Fong's head. It hung loosely around Fong's neck. Fong was about to continue but stopped and stood very still. His eyes hooded. His delicate fingers traced the circle of the noose around his neck. Then his hands were still and his eyes snapped open. Now, they were hard – angry. He barked, "Stop crying."

The girl looked up at him, wide-eyed.

Fong felt the loose rope around his neck again. "You did it, didn't you, Ophelia? Until now I only thought you lured Geoff here. That Laertes actually did the hanging. Now I know differently."

Before she could protest Fong charged on. "So Laertes looped the noose around Geoff's neck like Captain Chen just did around mine. But it's loose, isn't it Captain Chen?"

"Yes, it has to be to fit over your head."

"So Geoff does this." Fong straightened up and immediately reached for the noose. Chen leapt forward and fought with Fong to first tighten and then keep the noose on Fong's neck. Fong tries to loosen the noose but Chen held the knot tight. "The noose is now set, Ophelia, but Laertes literally has his hands filled keeping it on Geoff's neck. That being the case, who was left to pull the rope to hang Mr. Hyland?"

Ophelia stood. Her shoulders were back, her head held high. "He said I wasn't her. He said it was all a mistake. He said he was sorry." Suddenly she was screaming, "Sorry? Sorry? What the fuck does sorry mean?"

Fong weathered the verbal storm then counted to three before he asked, "Mr. Hyland said you weren't who?" Fong's voice was low. He dreaded but needed to hear the answer to his question.

"Her. Fu Tsong. Your wife, remember her?"

And there she was. A murderess. As if she had emerged from somewhere deep within the girl. A murderess with motive, means and opportunity – and more importantly – with the rage needed to kill a man she loved.

The formalities of arresting the two actors were handled by Captain Chen who quickly moved them out of the theatre to the waiting patrol car on Nanjing Lu.

Fong and Joan were alone. Fong went to the back of the

auditorium and sat in the exact same seat in which he'd last seen Geoff. Then sadly he said, "Fuck me with a stick."

"Is this a quaint Shanghanese phrase?" Joan asked as she moved up the aisle toward him. "Does it have an idiomatic meaning or is it to be taken literally?"

"In this case I probably deserve it literally."

"Being a bit hard on yourself, aren't you?"

"I don't think so."

Joan put a hand on her hip, sat on the arm of the theatre seat across the aisle from him and said, "Explanation, please."

He handed her the Shanghai detective's report of the dead woman found in the Su Zu Creek.

Joan read it quickly then looked at him. "And the key he found on the body fits . . . ?"

"It's the master key for the guesthouse that Mr. Hyland stayed in."

Joan thought about that for a moment. "How long was she dead before . . . ?"

"Impossible to say," Fong interrupted her. "The eels in the Su Zu Creek are ravenous."

"But she wasn't at the desk when you went to check Mr. Hyland's room the day after the murder?"

"No. The woman there was already complaining about how hard it was to keep new workers."

"So this poor woman was removed to be sure that no one could identify Ophelia as being with Mr. Hyland the night of the murder?"

"That would be my guess," Fong answered without much enthusiasm. "But when did they kill her? Before they killed Geoff or after, when . . . ?"

". . . when you could have . . . "

". . . done something about it if I had seen what was right in front of me. I allowed myself to be distracted by the little things and ignored the obvious."

"If that's true, it's very bad," she said flatly.

He looked at her. "Very bad," she repeated.

Fong nodded.

Joan reached up and tugged at a short blunt stand of hair. "So what exactly did you miss?"

"I missed the biggest clue that Geoff put in front of me."

"Which was?"

Fong almost laughed but didn't. Failure wasn't funny. Murder was certainly not a joke. He took a deep breath then let it out in a line – boy, he wanted a smoke. "The first thing Geoff made sure I saw was Laertes fight Hamlet who just happens to look like a young Geoff. Laertes clearly loves Ophelia. Ophelia loves Hamlet, Geoff. Geoff betrays Ophelia. Laertes and Ophelia kill Geoff. In the West they would say the table was all set for me. Here we'd say the fish's head faced me." He looked to Joan. "Do you think . . . ?"

". . . that the key lady would have lived if you'd understood what Mr. Hyland was trying to tell you?" She let out a long sigh. "No. I don't. The moment those two murdered Mr. Hyland that poor woman's fate was sealed. I assume it happened the same night. Once you kill a first time, the second is easier – especially if the second is a poor old woman."

Fong realized that he'd been holding his breath. He let it out in one long line of relief.

"That still leaves two things about the murder that are unaccounted for," said Fong.

"What two things?"

"The forget-me-nots in Geoff's pockets and the vest he wore on the hot night."

Joan smiled. "Neither strikes me as very mysterious."

"How do you mean?"

"Mr. Hyland was a middle-aged man having an affair with a young actress." She looked at Fong who gave no indication that he understood what she was getting at. "Come on, Fong!

Okay, I'll lay it out for you. In middle age, we all thicken Fong, don't we?" Fong nodded. "The vest helped Mr. Hyland cover that thickening, what Westerners call love handles." Joan raised her shoulders in the pan-Chinese gesture of "you-get-me?" then added, "How long can anyone hold their stomach in, anyway?"

Fong smiled. So the vest was nothing more than his old enemy, vanity, at work. "And the flowers?"

"Even easier, Fong."

"They are?"

"Yes, what are the flowers called, Fong?"

"Forget-me-nots."

"So there it is."

"There what is?"

Then she said the flower's name slowly – one word at a time – Forget – Me – Not. "Surely Ophelia put them in Mr. Hyland's pockets as a final memento, a final love token. A warning not to forget her."

Fong shook his head but smiled.

Joan got to her feet and her face turned dark. "There is however another mystery that strikes me as potentially far more sinister than anything to do with Mr. Hyland's death."

Fong nodded. He knew what she was going to say.

"Who told the two Beijing men that you'd planted a bug on Xi Luan Tu? It wasn't the snitch in the central stores. He worked for Li Chou."

This time Fong didn't even nod.

"Was it Captain Chen?" Joan asked.

Fong looked away.

It was almost midnight when Fong heard the knock on his office door. He'd been sitting in the dark lit only by the ambient light from the neon across the river in the Pudong. "It's open, Captain Chen."

The lights played chase-the-colour across the uncomely features of the young man as he entered the office and stood cap in hand. "Sir?"

Fong said nothing.

"You found out, sir?"

"Yes, Captain Chen, I found out. You betrayed me to the men from Beijing."

After a slight pause, Chen said, "I knew you would figure it out, sir."

"Then why did you do it?" Fong was on his feet. His voice was loud enough to rattle the glass in the window.

But Chen didn't flinch. "Because of Lily and Xiao Ming," he said simply. "This office is a political place. You told me that. I have to protect myself so that I can be there for Lily and Xiao Ming."

Fong looked at the young man. The colours seemed to float across the man's unfortunate features.

Then Fong nodded and turned to the window.

"Sir?"

"We all do what we need to do, Captain Chen." He reached up and touched the cool glass pane of the window. "All of us do what we need to do."

"Yes, sir."

A long silence followed. Captain Chen stood very still. Fong stared out at the Pudong. Then Fong turned to Chen. "I'll see you tomorrow morning, Captain Chen."

"Sir?"

"We understand each other now. I will see you tomorrow. We have work to do here, Captain Chen. Much work."

CHAPTER EIGHTEEN

ENDS AND BEGINNINGS

Fong opened the door to the safe house without knocking. The table in the centre of the room was covered with official-looking documents. A few of the mocked-up photographs were there of Geoff in handcuffs. The room's windows were all closed and curtained so the place was oppressively hot and stuffy despite the late hour. Fong threw open the draperies and pried open a window. It made little difference. Fong leaned out the window. Far-off he heard the gentle lap of the Huangpo River. Looking up, he thought he saw the moon about to set.

Fong checked the other rooms in the house. The elderly Beijing man wasn't there. Then he heard the front door open.

The politico with the large raspberry stain on his left cheek whom Fong had seen with the two French contractors in his courtyard, what seemed like years ago, strode into the room. The man hoisted a heavy briefcase onto the table and began to pack up the papers.

"Where's Sheng, the older man from Beijing?" Fong asked.

"Not here, evidently."

"Where is he?"

The politico looked up at Fong. "You know better than to ask something like that, Traitor Zhong."

Fong didn't reply.

The politico continued to pack his briefcase.

"Doesn't it ever bother you?" Fong asked, knowing full well it was better to keep his mouth shut – tight.

The man looked up from his packing. "No, it never bothers me, Traitor Zhong."

The single word *WHY* leapt out of Fong's mouth. But he wasn't really asking. He was falling. Begging for an answer. Lost.

The man on the other side of the table was Chinese like him. He was of flesh and would die like him. He probably loved and wanted and yearned like him – yet he did things that were beyond Fong's comprehension. Then, much to Fong's surprise, the man answered Fong's question. "Because, Traitor Zhong, we all need direction. It is wrong to believe that each of us wants to cut our own path. That each of us determines how and where we go. People like you have deluded yourselves into believing that your fellow citizens want to control their destiny. It is not true. It is not even remotely true. Most people, the vast majority of people, want to follow, not lead. They want to be led. We live, we follow, we die. Not hard to understand even for a person as confused as you, Traitor Zhong."

"And do we leave this world a better place?"

The man looked at Fong for a long moment, then finally said, "How can one possibly know such a thing?" He pushed one of the documents on the table toward Fong. "As chief investigator this requires your signature, just another one of the new formalities, our little step toward transparency."

The politico snapped his briefcase shut and then, without looking at Fong, turned and headed toward the front door of the safe house.

"People died here," Fong said to the Beijing man's back.

The Beijing man stopped for a beat, but he did not turn –

did not respond – just left Fong alone – with his thoughts and an empty room.

Fong grabbed the official document and sat. The new state font must have been reduced in size. He held it close but it remained just a blur. He tried it at full arm's-length – still no go. "Damn," he muttered as he reached into his coat pocket and put on his new glasses. The fog of dark strokes cleared and the shapes emerged as characters.

As he signed the document, Joan entered the room and sat opposite him.

"Nice haircut," Fong said.

Joan touched her ragged hair and shook her head. "How nice of you to finally notice. It makes me look Parisian, don't you think, Detective Zhong?"

Actually Fong didn't know from Parisian, nor did he care. Joan Shui's short hair simply allowed him a better view of the strength inherent in her face.

"I like you with glasses, Detective Zhong."

Fong had forgotten he still had them on. "Thanks."

"They make you look intelligent."

"Well, looking intelligent is something."

"Yes, it is. Let's get out of this place."

A half-hour later, Fong and Joan Shui stood side by side on the Bund Promenade looking across the Huangpo River at the Pudong as he finished telling her about his confrontation with Captain Chen.

"It was the right thing to do, Fong. Now you know where his loyalties lie. You know him well enough to work with him."

"I think so." A silence fell between them. The distance between her left hand and his right on the railing was a mere four inches – yet it could have been a mile or seven hundred miles.

"So what happens next?" Fong asked.

Joan wasn't sure exactly what he meant but chose to believe he was talking about her next professional move now that this "unpleasantness" was over. "Well," she said, "Shanghai's becoming a modern city. It'll need its own arson department soon enough. You folks can't always be calling over to old HK for help."

"That's true," he said – but nothing more.

Somehow their hands, despite the fact that neither had moved, seemed even farther apart – no longer a mile or seven hundred miles – now a light year or twenty.

She took a deep breath and made a decision. "I've been in love once before."

"With Wu Fan-zi."

"Yes, with Wu Fan-zi," she agreed. "What about you, Detective Zhong?"

"Once."

"But not with Lily?"

"No. To my shame, not with Lily." It was his turn to agree.

"With the actress?"

"Her name is Fu Tsong."

There it was. Wrong tense. She looked at his delicate features and suddenly she knew he'd done it on purpose. That he'd offered her an opening. Now she needed to figure out if she was brave enough to take it.

She was.

"You meant, her name *was* Fu Tsong."

Fong nodded slowly.

"She is too much with you, Fong."

Again Fong nodded. "I can't seem to let her go."

"Then don't. Just give her a place at the table, but not every seat, or the one to which the fish head points."

"Is that what you've done with Wu Fan-zi?"

Now it was her turn to nod.

"What place does he have at your table?"

She thought about that for only a moment then responded, "Fire. Every time my life becomes about fire Wu Fan-zi is at my side, alive as when he first touched me." She looked at the distance between their hands on the rail. "Can you do that with Fu Tsong?"

Fong didn't know. Then he looked into the depths of Joan Shui's eyes. "Yes, I think I can."

"How?" Joan's voice was hard. There was no movement in it. If Fong couldn't answer this she would take the next available flight back to Hong Kong and never again set foot in Shanghai or have any contact with the man who now stood beside her, his hand so close to hers on the railing, again.

"Fire with Wu Fan-zi and you, right? Art, especially theatre and Shakespeare for Fu Tsong and me."

"Only in those places?" she pressed.

"Only in those places."

There was a beat – a flutter of gulls moving in an arc high to the west – and the miracle happened. From light years apart hands met, fingers entwined and a sea breeze, all the way from the mighty Yangtze, blessed their coming together.

The darkness came on fast that evening. Time was moving quickly as Fong and Joan sought out a place to be alone – but privacy was the hardest thing to find in a city of 18 million souls.

"I would invite you back to my hotel but I have no room booked and no money on me to purchase one," Joan said.

He began to laugh.

She liked the sound and joined in. Their laughter grew until they staggered with the force of it. Passersby stopped and stared at them. Older people scolded. Finally Joan got enough control of herself to ask, "What are we laughing about?"

Fong answered through bursts of laughter that caused tears to roll down his cheeks, "I'll soon be in the same situation."

"What do you mean?"

"My rooms are going to be part of a new condominium project. They've offered me the right to buy them but . . . "

". . . but the price is a bit steep?"

"Yeah," Fong stopped laughing, "you could say that."

"Do you like these rooms, Fong?" she asked.

"I do."

Joan looked at the proud newness of the Pudong across the Huangpo River then turned and looked at the Bund behind her. It felt right. She touched Fong's face, "Would I like your rooms, do you think?"

Fong put his hand up to her hair and felt its bluntness, "I hope you would."

She put her lips to his and whispered into his mouth, "Ask me to your rooms, Fong."

Fong turned his head and whispered in her ear, 'Would you come with me to my rooms, Joan Shui?"

She whispered back into his ear, "I thought you'd never ask."